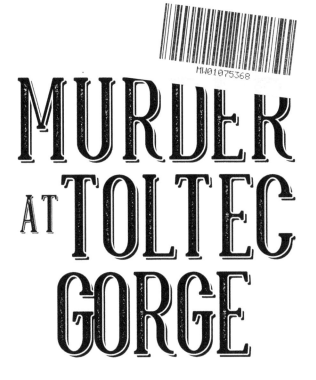

MURDER AT TOLTEC GORGE

A Denver & Rio Grande
Western Railroad Adventure

BILLY ANDERS

outskirts
press

1

DANGEROUS LOVE

Thursday, June 2, 1927. 8 am. At Antonito, Colorado, engineer Eliseo Martinez glanced up the track towards Lava Tank. By the time he drove the New Mexico Express by the tank's location, the passenger train would have gained 600 feet in elevation. On average, it was about a foot climb up for every 100 feet forward, a 1% grade. Very easy to deal with.

Eli, a Denver & Rio Grande Western employee since 1923, had made this trip often with his fireman, Samuel Gonzales. He knew how to manage his train's ascent. Time to go. Eli moved the throttle forward, causing steam to enter the steam cylinders on either side of the locomotive, setting the driving wheels in motion. He smoothly took up the slack between the cars. Eliseo Martinez was a very good engineer.

He sensed and understood the tremendous power of the living, breathing monster starting to move under his control, a balance of great force and synchronized moving parts teetering on the edge of disaster.

Engineer Martinez knew he should be 100%

focused on driving the train. But today, as usual of late, a portion of his mind was on the woman he loved. If he were lucky, he would see her in about an hour. Eli was engaged, in a family-arranged kind of way, to Maria Lopez. He and Maria had grown up near each other in Conejos, Colorado, and had attended the same church, Our Lady of Guadalupe, since they were children.

The engagement had been understood between the families for years, a planned thing. Everyone just knew they would be married. Maria was a nice girl, 20 years old, and was ready to start a family. Eli wasn't so sure, though.

Indeed, the woman on his mind whom he really loved wasn't Maria but someone else's wife. Her name was Arriana Garcia. She was married to Leo Garcia, the Sublette, New Mexico, section foreman for the Denver & Rio Grande Western railroad.

If public knowledge, nearly everyone would quickly say it was a dangerous situation. Eli knew better but couldn't seem to control his feelings.

2

THE WAR HERO
AND ARRIANA

The Express moved up the plateau at 12 miles per hour. Five miles into the 64 mile trip to Chama, the train crossed Ferguson's Trestle. About 1890, so the story went, one Mr. Ferguson of Antonito had committed a capital crime, the nature of which no one could remember. The local vigilante committee caught up with him and prepared for a hanging.

The problem with stringing anybody up in Antonito was that no tree of suitable height existed. So the committee commandeered a Denver & Rio Grande locomotive on which they took their prisoner and an appropriate rope to the trestle. The rope, when looped around the engine's chimney, could then cause the death of the said Mr. Ferguson by hanging, as his feet would not touch the ground when the engine was parked over the small bridge. Thus according to legend, Ferguson met his fate there.

Eli Martinez had often glanced to his left as his

climbing train crossed the trestle, contemplating the last view of Mother Earth that Ferguson once had. It was always a quiet moment of inner reflection. Eliseo wondered if someone in his current dilemma might unwittingly gain the same destiny. If so, and he hoped not, at least he would not be the trailblazer!

Today he was driving engine # 489. The '89 was a beautiful machine, only two years old, built by the Baldwin Locomotive Works of Philadelphia, Pennsylvania. She'd cost $28,000, a huge sum. She carried 5,000 gallons of water and wouldn't need to fill up at Lava Tank, where the water came up more than 2,000 feet from the Rio de Los Pinos, the River of the Pines. The locomotive's tender held nine and one-half tons of coal, more than enough to make the entire trip.

The 480 series of locomotives, also called the K-36 model, had been designed with all the knowledge of 50 years of mountain railroading in mind and was the finest of its kind.

It was a bit unusual for the '89 to be leaving Antonito pulling the New Mexico Express passenger train. She was typically assigned as helper getting heavy freights up the 'big hill' from Chama, New Mexico, to Cumbres Pass, Colorado. Today's job usually went to a K-27 or K-28, smaller engines. But engine # 489 had been to the Antonito shops for a needed part, had been repaired, and it made no sense to run her light back to Chama. So here she was.

Mr. Alvie Johnson lived at the pump house near the Rio de Los Pinos, had for years. He kept the water full in Lava Tank. It was a lonely job, but one at which Alvie was an expert. He'd know from the whistle sound as well as from the train orders and schedule which engine was going by with what train, and would know that a big K-36 like the '89 wouldn't take on water until it got to Sublette. It would also travel through Big Horn, the next section gang location, before stopping. Alvie, like Eli and fireman Sam Gonzales, was a professional who knew his job well.

The '89 rolled on. San Antonio Peak, 10,935 feet tall, was on the left. It still had an active vent but hadn't said or done much for the last few million years. The basalt it had emitted back then in a kind, gentle sort of way – for a volcano – was layered across the landscape. The twin peaks of Los Mogotes volcano stood on the right. Its name translated to "The Horns of Small Animals."

About 28 million years ago, Los Mogotes had violently erupted, leaving a caldera, and all these black lava rocks spread around. Like San Antonio Peak, it had spoken its piece and was happy to stay silent. That would have pleased both train crew and passengers if anyone had thought of it today.

Big Horn section house was coming up on the right. That section crew hadn't been sighted along the track they maintained, leaving Eli and Sam to believe it might be their mealtime. Eli blew the whistle announcing his arrival, again not a surprise to the folks at Big Horn. They'd have been more surprised not to hear it.

The train lumbered on westward, now doing 14 miles per hour once above the plateau and the initial climb. They went around Whiplash Curve, then looked down on the Three Ply, three levels of track they'd just navigated upwards in a way the locomotive could make its climb at a reasonable rate.

Passengers often wondered about the turning and twisting, and indeed it was said that when the San Juan

Extension was built back in 1880, the survey crew had just turned their mule loose and herded him up the mesa, knowing the animal would pick the most natural way of gaining the summit with the least effort. It probably wasn't a true story, but it had a certain logic.

Pinon and juniper flew by as the train pushed on. There was a wider variety of vegetation now, the big sagebrush and smaller rabbitbrush known by locals as 'chamiso' having been mostly left behind at lower elevations. On the right, at milepost 278, Eli spied the 10,000-year-old petroglyph of a thunderbird carved on a large boulder, near the crest of a ridge, underneath a prominent ponderosa pine.

Eli liked to think that an ancient Anasazi had been waiting for the New Mexico Express and had been bored – and with time on his hands, he'd carved this picture of a bird.

A few more curves around the gigantic north side of the Rio de Los Pinos canyon brought Eli's train close to Sublette, New Mexico. Sublette was home to the next section gang past Big Horn that took care of another seven miles of track. Foreman Leo Garcia, the husband of Arriana Garcia, was around someplace. Leo had a tough job, but he was a tough hombre.

Leo stood 6 feet 4 inches tall and weighed 240 pounds, none of it fat. He had an outstanding record with the Denver & Rio Grande Western. Starting at age 16, Leo worked on this very same gang for two years. He knew the job inside and out.

While Leo first worked for the railroad, World War I came along. The United States declared war on Germany after Germany announced unrestricted submarine warfare on US ships. The US Army was small.

President Wilson called for volunteers, thinking that patriotism alone would produce the required results. It did not. Colorado's State Guard was activated and provided more than 4,000 troops, but more soldiers were needed. Military conscription, a draft, was put in place. Another 4,800 males were called up and sent to national training camps. Leo Garcia was one of the draftees. He was then 19 years of age.

After training, Garcia was sent to France, placed on the front lines with fellow members of the 82nd Division. Trench warfare was the order of the day. It was brutal; casualty rates were incredible. Leo Garcia was big and strong, facilitating his promotion to Corporal. No dummy, he was quick to see that going 'over the top' of the trench first was a fast ticket to an early death.

German machine gunners sighted in the American positions. At the order to charge, the gunners opened up, and as many as half the soldiers trying to advance were almost immediately cut down. Those who weren't killed but seriously wounded created the additional problem of rescue.

Leo did not expect to survive but wisely learned for his benefit that it was best to hold back a second or two while he rallied those of his platoon to get out of the trench and on with it.

Doing so gave him some cover that others didn't have - the bodies of his comrades. He stayed down and only carefully exposed himself to enemy fire, staying in a belly-down low crawl, using the corpses of others in his unit for protection.

His commanders didn't notice so much his method of survival as the very fact he did when others did not. He was sent on a special mission with 15 fellow soldiers. They were to infiltrate German lines and conduct surveillance on enemy unit strength and placement. Another primary purpose was to take out a German machine-gun position that was wreaking havoc on American troops.

Alvin York, a fellow Corporal and a farm boy from Tennessee was another of the group chosen. York, although religious, was a drinker and brawler when the opportunity presented itself. He and Leo had become pals during such activity, backing each other up.

On the battlefield, the 16 Americans went forward, capturing a large number of German soldiers, but were counterattacked. Six of their own were killed and another three wounded.

Alvin York took charge, and Leo, still among the living, didn't argue with him. The leader was more likely to be targeted. York detailed Leo and the others to guard the prisoners, then he attacked the machine gun position. Corporal York killed several of the enemy with his A-1903 Springfield rifle before running out of ammunition. Six Germans rushed York, who then drew his A-1911 Browning .45 semi-automatic pistol and killed all six.

The German soldier in charge of the position emptied his pistol at York, missing with every round, and then surrendered his unit to Corporal York, who accepted the surrender. Alvin York and the others, including Leo, marched more than 130 prisoners back to the 82nd. Immediately, York put on Sergeant stripes as a reward, and Leo Garcia's promotion to that rank wasn't far down the road.

For his actions, Sergeant Alvin C. York received the Distinguished Service Cross, soon upgraded to the

Medal of Honor, the highest combat decoration given by the US military.

Sergeant Leo Garcia and five others received the Bronze Star, the nation's fourth-highest medal for bravery for their part in the action. Sergeant Garcia became a military hero while serving in France.

Something else happened to Leo 'over there'. He took seriously the lyrics of the famous World War I song, "How you gonna keep 'em down on the farm, when they've seen Paree?". On rare leaves from his unit, Leo and his buddies traveled to Paris or other cities and were regulars at brothels where they drank and raised hell. Consorting with the pretty French prostitutes changed Leo for the worse, and he was already big and tough and mean. Now he enjoyed flaunting his strength by slapping the girls around and otherwise mistreating them. That sort of behavior added to his enjoyment of the sexual thrill.

Leo was from Alamosa, just north of Antonito. He returned home, a genuine hero, to a big welcome. The economy in the United States would be slow for two years after the November 11, 1918, armistice ended World War I. But it soon picked up as soldiers rejoined the workforce and factories retooled from wartime production to consumer goods. Leo didn't have to wait for employment, though. After being feted in Alamosa, he was immediately offered his choice of jobs. The Denver & Rio Grande Western Railroad needed a tough foreman for the Sublette section gang where he'd previously worked. He had the background, and he had the inside knowledge. He hired on right away.

But he'd seen gay Paree. He'd liked what he'd seen.

He wanted a woman. And he wanted a pretty one. Just what a war hero deserved. Enter Arriana Espinoza.

The Espinoza family was also from Alamosa. Mr. Espinoza had worked for the Denver & Rio Grande as a laborer, helping build the line between Antonito and Durango. He knew that a foreman with the railroad had a bright future. Times were good and getting better. The railroad was making money and, during 1924, had ordered ten new Baldwin K-36 locomotives, which were delivered as soon as they rolled off the assembly line.

Mr. Espinoza and his wife faced another situation. They had four children, all girls. Arriana was the oldest. The middle two were already married. The youngest was promised to someone. But Arriana was still at home. Why?

Arriana Espinoza was beautiful. She had long black hair, a beautiful face, and a slender build. Arri was intelligent and a good cook and had homemaker skills. But she wasn't perfect. One leg, her right, was shorter than the other. She walked with a definite limp. Prospective suitors had been scared away. In her neighborhood, Arriana was the "but" girl. "She's beautiful," they would say, "but she has a disability. She limps and won't get over it." *No one will want her,* they were thinking. *For one thing, she may have a great many medical expenses.*

A doctor from Denver had been traveling through Alamosa one day when she and her family were at the Denver & Rio Grande Western depot to meet a relative. The doctor noticed both her beauty and her disability and offered to examine her. Osteomyelitis was his diagnosis. Bed rest for up to a year with lots of sunshine, with Vitamin D from food like carrots, was his pre-scription. Arriana stayed in bed for most of the year and sometimes lay outside in the sun, plentiful in the San Luis Valley, at least in the summertime. She ate what Vitamin D-rich foods her family could afford. At best, she didn't get worse, but finally tired of the 'cure' and just went on with life.

Leo's family had told him that if he wanted a faith-ful, hard-working woman, he should find someone in the church. One weekend he went to a religious festival in Alamosa and saw Arriana. Her good looks impressed him. He thought, *here's a beautiful woman, and with her physical disability, there won't be so many men interested in taking her away from me.*

There were things Leo Garcia disregarded, however, if he thought of them at all. Times were changing in the United States, and women were changing with them. They'd gotten the vote in 1920. Magazines and movies and newspapers were encouraging women to become different from the way Leo perceived them. And they were becoming more independent. But he liked them the way they had been, loved having power over them. He enjoyed having slapped the French girls around.

After the festival, Garcia inquired about Arriana through a mutual friend. Mr. Espinoza, told of Leo's interest, was more than happy to give his blessing for the union. And why not?

Leo was a genuine war hero. He had a good job. He had a nice home in Sublette that Mr. Espinoza remem-bered helping build when constructing the line. Leo and Arriana married in 1923. They moved to Sublette. In addition to her regular chores as Leo's wife and home-maker, her job was to cook for the 12 men of the section gang, three meals a day. The men ate those meals in the dining room of Arriana's home. It was a great deal of work, but Arri tried to remain positive and count her blessings. Their only connection with the outside world was the train.

It was a while before the mistreatment of Arri by Leo began, but when it did start, it started with a passion.

Those slips and falls around the house that caused black eyes and other bruises seemed to become commonplace. To the casual observer, it would seem that Arriana was a very clumsy person. The section gang members may have been uneducated, ordinary men, but they had common sense, weren't stupid. It wasn't long before the bunkhouse gossip started, but it was kept to a very low level. Foreman Garcia was one mean rascal who ruled not only his household through force and intimidation but his section gang as well, in that same manner. If one valued his job – and maybe his physical well-being – it wasn't wise to speak up in any way or to challenge the boss.

And the railroad was very happy with the work produced by the gang under foreman Leo Garcia, formerly Sergeant Garcia, the war hero.

Life chugged along.

3

A DELICATE BALANCE

A section man's job was a hard one. Living and working conditions were brutal. It was work for a young man, usually his first job. He walked several miles out and back each day along the line, carrying a maul to nail down spikes, and a track wrench. As he walked, he inspected the track and pounded in any loose spikes. He used the wrench to tighten rail joiners and did any other maintenance that he could do alone. With two men walking in opposite directions, they checked their area of responsibility in its entirety daily.

If any materials were needed to make repairs along the route, they would be put on a push car and pushed to the worksite by hand by the section men. Now and then, the push car might be attached to the end of a train and towed to the place needing work. Most men stayed at Sublette for about two years, then moved on. Often moving along was to a better job with the railroad. Working for foreman Leo Garcia was especially demanding, but life wasn't a bed of roses for young men anywhere, and most were already used to harsh conditions, so they tolerated such things.

Leo Garcia was as robust as any of them and had done their job when he was their age, so he expected them to buck up and take it. He tolerated no slackness, no weakness, no bellyaching about the cold, or the long hours. His responsibility was to see that seven miles of track was maintained. Since he was a professional, that was going to happen under his watch.

Leo Garcia was a big man, and if someone was unwise enough to stand up to him, he wasn't beyond belting that man into submission. When others saw that, they fell into line pretty quickly, as a general rule. Occasionally a new man showed up for work who bowed his neck at Leo, but such behavior was brought under control fast, or the man lost his job. Mr. Hawkins, the Chama division superintendent, liked Leo. So Leo's decisions as foreman were nearly always upheld, and the men knew it. If a man wanted to keep his job, Leo's behavior was tolerated, or the man left, and someone else was hired to take his place.

Guillermo Estrada was one of the dozen working under Leo. Estrada was known to everyone as Willie. He wasn't retarded but had been born slow. Both oars were in the water, but one was a little deeper than the other. He was a willing worker, though, who did his job. He never argued and was glad to have work because no one else had offered him any. At age 21, things had looked pretty desperate for Willie until railroad employment came along.

Foreman Garcia didn't have to bully Willie because Willie happily did whatever Leo told him to do. There was never a thought of disagreeing with the foreman.

Mr. Garcia was the boss, and that was that. The other men might sometimes engage in bunkhouse talk at night in quiet disagreement with the foreman's way of getting work done, but such talk stayed in the bunkhouse. Well, the bunkhouses. There were two at Sublette, with six men living in each.

Occasionally a man might be switched from one to the other. It had happened recently when three men in one bunkhouse complained that Evan Morales snored so much and so loud that they couldn't sleep. Since Leo could see they were tired at the start of the day, he agreed that Shorty – everyone called Evan Morales that since he was 5 feet 2 inches tall, or short one might say – should sleep in the other bunkhouse and see how that worked out. Two men in the additional bunkhouse had recently argued over a family matter harkening back to their hometown, so Leo thought it wise to shift one to different sleeping quarters before something got out of hand.

The gang thought of Willie as simple, but he had never betrayed a confidence, so he was well-liked. He never complained about tough assignments and always pulled his share of the load. No one believed that he was playing up to the foreman. Everyone knew that Willie was just like that and that it would be hard for him to find other work.

The men were young, and naturally, they saw that Leo Garcia's wife, Arriana, was a real beauty. It would be hard for a man with two eyes or even one not to notice. Sometimes there was hushed bunkhouse gossip about her between two men who trusted each other, but it was never an open topic of conversation. All the men firmly believed that if foreman Garcia heard anyone saying anything about his wife, more than just a firing might take place. Death might be your fate. The men knew that Leo Garcia had killed many men in the war and didn't think he'd hesitate to do that without thinking about consequences, and they believed it was even likely it would be covered up if he did.

Much of their work happened in high, dangerous settings, and an accident would be easily explained, especially if a man were helping the foreman at a place out of sight of the others. Even without provoking the boss, it was a risky job. So any talk of Mrs. Garcia's unusual beauty was low key, private conversation.

Another topic treated with discretion centered around the fairly frequent occasions when Arriana Garcia appeared with an injury - a black eye, bruises on her arms, or face. The gang men were young, but they were alert and observant. Some of them had seen the harsh treatment of women at home, usually their mother or sometimes a sister who was 'acting out' according to their father. Hard physical handling of women wasn't that unusual or shocking.

But women in the United States were beginning to behave differently than in the past. Getting the vote in 1920 was a significant accomplishment. Many girls back east were called Flappers because of their lifestyle. Flappers believed in more independence, having jobs, living more freely. They were even expressing their attitudes towards sex more openly. During World War I, many females had taken the place of men in factories who were called into military service. They'd given up those jobs when the men returned home but not the new feelings about the freedom they'd developed.

While much of this movement happened outside

southern Colorado or northern New Mexico, women in those places were reading about such changes in magazines and books and newspapers. Women like actress Clara Bow, the "It Girl," were openly pushing for change in movies in which they appeared. Women were beginning to think for themselves, even if mostly to themselves.

In 1927, another popular actress, Mae West, a big box office success, likewise advocated a 'do your own thing' philosophy. Famous for her line in a movie, "Come on up and see me sometime!", Mae West talked candidly about sex, and movie fans were fascinated by her frank behavior.

Change was coming.

4

GETTING BELTED

The truth was, like Denver & Rio Grande Western locomotive engineer Eliseo Martinez, every man in the section gang of Leo Garcia was in love with Leo's wife to some degree, thought about her secretly. Arriana Garcia wasn't just pretty; she had a good heart. She certainly didn't openly express any feelings towards the men, but she was kind to them. Arri fed them well, took care to cook unique desserts that the men liked, especially on their birthday. She made a note of each man's special day and made sure to remember and celebrate it, at least in a small way.

Being fussed over was something the men found unusual, so even a small remembrance was noteworthy. Therefore, Mrs. Garcia was vital to them. The fact that she had that limp from having a disease young in life made no difference at all. Besides, they were on their version of a desert island. It was a lonely, isolated world, and she was the only woman in it, at least the only one who wasn't passing through on a train. Mrs. Garcia was the lone female who stayed for more than a few minutes except for the rare times a train broke down at Sublette or harsh winter conditions like snow or ice interfered with the schedule.

Leo Garcia didn't like his wife making a treat for a man on his birthday, but cooking was her job, and if such behavior kept the men happy and working hard, he didn't think it wise to stop her. A good cook was hard to find, and his choices limited, primarily to her.

Willie Estrada was especially fascinated with Arriana Garcia. Willie, being simple, was the only one of the men that got an occasional smile from Arri. She knew it wasn't wise to favor any of them with a direct look as she understood they were young men who were eager to know women in a personal way and would likely misunderstand. But Willie was different and had never been treated uniquely before, so a thankful look from him meant something to Arriana. When Willie had time, he would help her move coal from the coal shed to the big box by the kitchen stove.

The shed was 50 feet from the section house, and it was no easy chore to keep the coal box full. It was placed conveniently to the tracks and snow trains that needed coal, not to be handy for the cook. So 50 feet away, it stayed. She'd give Willie a quiet smile when he took his limited time off to help her, and Willie's heart would melt. The other men saw that, but they all liked him, and jealousy didn't rear its ugly head. They knew it wouldn't go further and weren't bothered by it, though each of them would have liked to have a smile for himself. Of course, each understood it would possibly be the kiss of death if they'd gotten that smile, and foreman Garcia had seen it.

Willie Estrada was poor as were near all the men.

When he started working for Leo Garcia and began doing favors for Mrs. Garcia, she'd noticed that Willie only had a piece of rope for a belt. With an expanding belly, Leo had a good leather belt he'd outgrown, and it was useless to Leo. So Arriana asked him if she could give it to Willie for a birthday present. Leo Garcia would have rejected her request on behalf of any other gang worker but saw no harm in it since Willie was not a threat in any way and was loyal to Leo. So he said yes. Willie wore that belt from then on with a great deal of gratitude and pride.

Leo had forgotten that Arri had given him the belt as a wedding present. It was engraved "From Arriana with love" on the backside. The other men teased Willie about that, though they knew the words had been for Leo, and Willie just smiled when they did. He liked to think of it as a special message to him from Mrs. Garcia.

Willie Estrada, too, saw the bruises and black eyes of Arriana Garcia. He was simple but smart enough to leave his observations unspoken. He loved getting her unique look, even if something as unpleasant as those injuries framed it. Like the rest of the men, though, Willie saw but wisely said nothing. It was a pot that no man wanted to stir.

The trains passing through both eastbound and westbound brought news of the outside world. They dropped off magazines and newspapers, and even books that were left by passengers during brief stops. The train crew, all of them male, and all of them secretly as much in love with the beautiful but untouchable Arriana Garcia as any of the section gang, gave her special treatment. When she needed groceries or other supplies, she gave her list to someone going east on the train. The railroad maintained charge accounts for her at Antonito stores. Supplies were returned within 24 hours by a westbound train.

The westbound train was officially called the New Mexico Express, the eastbound train the Colorado Express. But those names were mainly the railroad's promotion of its services, and something fancy for The Public. To the people living and working at Sublette, it was merely the Westbound or the Eastbound passenger train.

Everything considered, the world of the Sublette section gang was a place of productive work but was a dangerous one, held together with the glue of both certainty and uncertainty.

5

WHISTLE WHILE YOU WORK

In June 1927, it wasn't quite summertime, but the weather was warmer, and snow was gone for the next few months. Now and then, a thunderstorm would cool things off up to 30 or 40 degrees, and there might even be hail. But it wouldn't stick to the ground, stay around as ice and snow did. So the weather was good, as good as it was likely to get. The rainy season, the time of monsoons, would come in July and August, and it would be hottest then, sometimes reaching 90 degrees in the daytime, but even then, the humidity was tolerable and the heat not unbearable.

Arri enjoyed walking alone occasionally, and she justified those walks by gathering wild berries to use in the food she cooked. It was a great time to relax a little, to think of the life she was living, to maybe even secretly wish for better things. As a young girl, like all young girls, she had dreamed of being in love, of being treated lovingly by a good husband, of being happy.

Life, it seemed, hadn't worked out quite that way.

But Arri understood the conditions of the day, of her place in the world she called home. She read the stories in newspapers and books and magazines of changes that were coming. Of course, she kept such stories well hidden from Leo. Did she want to be involved in those changes? She pondered that question. She was old-fashioned enough to know she didn't wish to have a spear in her hands, throwing it for women's rights. But if women altogether had a new spear, she thought it would be nice to have her hand on the handle. She looked at her mother's life and thought she'd like an improvement on that lifestyle for her own.

During her walks, she sometimes traveled as far as a half-mile to the west, to an old black powder magazine. It had been built during railroad construction in 1880 to hold the dangerous but useful explosive used extensively.

The magazine faced away from the community of Sublette, so if it blew up, the force of the blast would not harm the people who lived there. The safer explosive, dynamite, had been available in 1880, but there was a surplus of black powder left over from the Civil War. It was cheaper, and there were plenty of Civil War 'powder monkeys' – men trained in its use – around to hire. The cost of railroad construction, though no one might say it outside a boardroom, was more important than the lives of a few workers. So black powder was utilized along the railroad.

In June of 1927, though, Arri Garcia wasn't thinking about those things as she walked over to the old powder magazine that had the appearance of a mine shaft. She'd go directly, doing her berry picking on the way back home. Arriana would take a few minutes, whatever time could be spared though it wasn't much, to sit and lean back against the magazine door. She especially liked going there on sunny days. The doctor who'd diagnosed her osteomyelitis said the sun would be healthy for her.

Sitting there, she'd mull things over. Though there was no one she could talk to about it, her thoughts might turn to what she wanted to believe about marriage and love. She'd always wanted to be made love to, to be a part of that, to be a willing partner. "Wham bam, thank you ma'am" she'd read once in a story, and she'd smile inwardly, thinking that was how it seemed to be in spite of her wishes. Two of the section gang men were very handsome. Sometimes one of their faces would slip into her thoughts, which would frighten her, and she'd force those faces to leave, turning a little red in the process.

But there was a face that would appear, and she wouldn't tell it to leave. One day she'd walked to the coal shed to fetch coal when the Westbound was pulling in. One luxury she had was a pair of shoes that had a lift in the right one to help her walk better. It was her only such pair, and she wore them sparingly, saving them for significant occasions. She happened to have them on that day, just as a lark.

Engineer Eliseo Martinez eased the Westbound to a stop at Sublette as Mrs. Garcia walked to the shed. The train stopped with the tender beneath the water fill spout. The water flowed from a spring on the hillside above Sublette to the cistern that held it.

There was some problem with a truck – a wheel and axle set – at the right rear of the consist, that day being six cars. Eliseo had paid quiet attention to Arriana Garcia at Sublette for some time now. And had developed special feelings for her, he thought, feelings that could be serious. Eli told Samuel Gonzales, the fireman, to go back and help with the mechanical problem. Sam wasn't stupid. He'd seen Arriana Garcia and had sensed Eli's interest in her. He gave Eli a warning look, which said don't do it, Eli, don't talk to her. The Westbound had passed the section gang three miles to the east, and both knew that Leo Garcia was away from Sublette, having seen him out that direction.

But love has no bounds, and Eli recognized an opportunity when he saw one. Arriana carefully avoided eye contact with both the fireman and engineer as she approached the little building. She thought she might have liked to have made eye contact with the engineer whom she'd noticed previously but knew better.

Though daylight, the light in the closed shed was subdued even with the door standing open. Eli had once again taken note of her great beauty as he watched her walk. Her face and even her limp always had stirred up his love-afflicted heart, and he truly wanted to help her.

Eli walked through the coal shed door as Arri Garcia turned to exit. In the near darkness, their faces almost came into contact as they both stopped abruptly. Eli saw her up close for the first time. Her eyes drew him to her, even in the subdued light. They were a mysterious blue-green color. To Eliseo, they seemed to have an indescribable magical, almost mystical quality.

Eli felt his heart do a flip-flop. He was momentarily dizzy. Arriana Garcia recognized the happening for what it was. Eli Martinez was attracted to her, had feelings for her, she knew. Both stammered in an attempt to say something, anything.

Finally, the moment passed, but not the feeling. Arri backed up a step, tried to walk around Eli, who blocked the door, though intentionally blocking the door wasn't in his game plan. He was just powerless to move. Finally, his heart stopped its revolution, and some thought of actually speaking came into his head.

He apologized. "I'm sorry, Mrs. Garcia. I thought you might need some help with getting the coal back to your house. May I help you?" His eyes were a little hazy. Arri was embarrassed to have made this man that she secretly fantasized about experience discomfort. She knew better, but it was 1927 even in Sublette, New Mexico, wasn't it? A new day. And her husband said he'd be working three miles out on the line to the east until dark. Why not?

She nodded yes and set out for the section house, still that 50 feet away. Her newly acquired love slave, Eli Martinez, was in tow, carrying the coal bucket. They stopped at the kitchen door, and Arri took the pail. Eli, racking his brain, suddenly had an idea, a way they could communicate without appearing to communicate.

"Mrs. Garcia, thank you for letting me help you. When we approach a station, the railroad requires that we sound two long notes and one short note on the whistle. Each engineer follows that rule, but we're allowed to modify it some for our unique sound. I've heard your name sometimes shortened to Arri. From now on, so that you know it's me, and since you know I am willing to help you get coal, I will always sound my whistle like this on the first long note: AaaaaaaaaaahRiiiiiiiiiiiiiiiiiiii! When you hear that, and if you would like your bucket filled, just set it out by your back door. I will either fill it myself or send Sam or another of the train crew. We appreciate what you do and would like to help."

Arriana Garcia then committed what for her would be a gesture she could never take back, that indeed no matter how brazen it was in the moment, she would never take back. She gave Eli Martinez a big smile, said, "Thank you, Mr. Martinez!" and turned and went inside. She had made a secret alliance with a man, not her husband.

In the bright daylight by the door, those mystical eyes captivated Eli. They reeled him in like a hooked fish. Of course, he had no intention of letting anyone besides Eli Martinez fill Mrs. Garcia's coal bucket, except for Willie Estrada, whom he knew already helped her sometimes. He wouldn't be jealous of Willie because he liked him, as did everyone.

Sam Gonzales returned to the cab. He saw a strange glow on Eli's face. Sam knew something had happened, but what? Eli looked away. "Fire her up, Sam! Let's get out of here." He wouldn't look directly at Sam. As Eli released the brakes and prepared to proceed, he was required to make two prolonged blasts on the whistle. *Might as well start using my new sound now,* he thought, *and get her used to it.*

On the first note, Sam heard a mysterious, different long sound he'd never heard before. AaaaaaaaahRiiiiiiiiiiiiiiiiiiiii! Sam looked at Eli, very curious. After several years of blowing the whistle one way – every engineer had his signature sound – he'd changed? Hmmm. Later, for sure, he would figure out it was code for Arri, but it didn't fully dawn on him at the time.

Someone else heard it, someone who was also familiar with all the usual whistle signatures. Arriana Garcia was stoking her stove with the coal that Eli had carried. She blushed. Stoked herself, it seemed, she felt a warm glow never experienced before in her life. It wasn't ever to go away.

Westbound, Eli couldn't get those eyes out of his mind.

6

RUNNING AND SMILING

Leo returned from his job to the east, bringing his crew with him. They'd had a productive workday. He and the men ate supper, then the section gang workers returned to their separate bunkhouses, save Willie, who hung around a few minutes to help Mrs. Garcia. He cleared the table and put the dishes in the sink. No problem for Leo with that, he was used to Willie fawning over his wife. It meant nothing. Just the silliness of a simple man.

He knew that Willie was harmless. He didn't have to bully him like the others, ride the hard kind of shotgun on him. Whatever foreman Garcia told Willie to do, Willie did. Once Leo had been mad at the crew for being what he called lazy, not working hard enough. A freight train became stuck as a result of work on the siding they hadn't finished on time. In a rare chastising from Mr. Hawkins, the division superintendent at Chama, the Sublette foreman had been humiliated. He'd gathered the men and read them the riot act. He'd so scared Willie that Willie Estrada had taken off for someplace immediately afterward, and hadn't come back until noon the next day.

"Why, Willie?" asked Garcia when Estrada returned, considering whether to fire him. "Where were you?"

Willie explained that he'd been scared nearly to death by what Mr. Garcia had said and had slept in the woods overnight. With daylight, he finally got the courage to return. Leo Garcia realized then he had complete power over Willie Estrada and decided to make a rare exception in the way he disciplined Willie compared to the way he strictly controlled the others. There was no need to scold him or physically touch him to get complete compliance.

It seemed to Leo that evening after supper that Arri was a little perkier than usual. *Fine,* he thought, *she's got energy, I want to take her tonight, it will be energy well spent.* As was his habit, to hell with foreplay, *I've been to gay Paree and know how to treat women.* In spite of rough treatment, *let's do this and get it over with,* Arri seemed to respond with a new mood of enthusiasm, though she kept her eyes closed. A sound ran through her head. AaaaaaaaaaahRiiiiiiiiiiiiiiiiiiiiii!

Women, Leo thought, *who can figure them. Oh well, wham bam, thank you, ma'am, I'm out of here. I got what I wanted.*

Life continued at Sublette, with one minor difference. One railroad engineer had changed his signature whistle. "Just wanted to do something different," said Eli.

"Yeah, sure, boss," said Sam.

A certain lady had developed a secret signature smile whenever she heard it, glancing up to see a particular engineer as she placed a coal bucket outside her back door.

7

GOOD TIMES

Times were good for the Denver & Rio Grande Western in 1927. General William Jackson Palmer chartered the line during 1870 in Denver, Colorado. His idea was to build to El Paso, Texas, then on to Mexico City. Other railroads had completed or were seeking transcontinental routes across the United States to the Pacific Ocean.

General Palmer probably had the same idea in mind, with access to ocean trade coming through the Mexican port of Vera Cruz. He laid out Colorado Springs, first called Fountain Springs. The railroad reached that new town in 1872. It took six more years to get to Alamosa where flowed the Rio Grande, the railroad finally achieving its namesake. In another two years, it was at Antonito, another new town established by the Denver & Rio Grande, the company's name before "Western" was added in one of a series of reorganizations.

Railroads were ruthless in their pursuit of profits and bypassed any city or town that didn't play along with their demands for property and other concessions, like tax credits. Conejos, Colorado, was one such place.

So Antonito was established just a mile south. Conejos was soon in decline.

The United States had ended its involvement in World War I with the armistice signed at Versailles, France, in November of 1918. Factories in the US that had retooled for war production then had to refit for civilian consumer goods production. The country was two years in recovering economically, but when it did, it did royally, and times were prosperous. They would remain so until 1929 when a worldwide economic slowdown started the Great Depression, but in 1927 no one saw that coming.

As a highly trained and proficient railroad engineer, Eli Martinez was one of the people enjoying relative prosperity. He had a fiancée, Maria Lopez, courtesy of his family's matchmaking, but the discovery of true love, though hidden, with Arri Garcia finally persuaded Eli to end the relationship. Maria was a nice girl, and it wasn't fair to keep stringing her along.

And Eli had learned through friends that a young man in Conejos, younger than Eli, was very interested in pursuing a relationship with Maria. His name was Joseph Alonzo. He came from a good family and was just a year older than Maria. Young love. Eli was by now 28. Why not end the relationship and give Joseph a chance? The timing seemed right.

Eli was living in Conejos near his parents. He'd bought a small house and had fixed it up nicely. There was a neighborhood dance that Eliseo attended with Maria on one of his weekends off work. He called her outside.

Eli told Maria that he was sorry, but both of them should have the chance to choose whom they wanted to marry and not have the issue forced on them by their parents. She took the supposedly bad news with a more carefree grace than Eli would have preferred for his dignity, but mission accomplished. It hurt his feelings a bit more than he thought it would because it didn't seem to hurt Maria's feelings much at all. Each told their parents the next day, and while the families were disappointed, they'd get over it.

Eli, of course, could not reveal his attraction to Arri Garcia, a married woman whose husband was a local war hero. Only his locomotive whistle could mention her name, and only Arriana could appreciate that sound. Sam Gonzales, Eli's regular fireman soon figured it out, though Eli wouldn't admit it to Sam for some time to come. Sam began to notice the coal bucket outside Arri's kitchen door when Eli's whistle signaled for it. Their system became clear to him one day when he was firing for another engineer, that engineer's different signature whistle sounded, and the coal bucket didn't appear. *So that's the way it is,* he thought.

Sam hoped that Leo Garcia didn't tune in to train whistles and coal buckets with the same insight.

It wasn't long before Maria and Joseph were engaged, both very happy with the arrangement. In a year, they would marry. Joseph, meanwhile, went to work for the Denver & Rio Grande Western at the Antonito depot as a baggage handler and would toil for the railroad for many years after that.

Maria and Joseph would have their first baby, a boy, within a year of marriage, and the child would be named Eliseo in thanks to the man who gave up Maria, to make Joseph so happy.

Go figure.

8

SUBLETTE, A FUR PIECE

In the late 1870s, while the Denver & Rio Grande was being built south towards El Paso and Mexico City, silver ore was discovered in the San Juan Mountains, west of Antonito. General Palmer smelled money, the main commodity that interested the railroad. The track continued south almost to Santa Fe – the Chili Line - but the San Juan Extension was formed to go west, young railroad, go west. It had reached Antonito by March of 1880.

Surveyors, track graders, and tie and rail workers headed west from Antonito on March 31, 1880. It took only nine months to reach Chama, New Mexico, on December 31, 1880. Speed was felt to be essential. The Atchison, Topeka & Santa Fe, the Denver & Rio Grande's chief competitor, was coming up from the south to reach that same money.

Section gang settlements were established along the way, and when the railroad completed facilities to each of those points, the line opened for business. Sublette was in place by May of 1880. It was first called

Boydsville for reasons no one could recall. Most likely, it had been named after some company official.

William Sublette, part-owner of the American Fur Trading Company, was one of five brothers from St. Louis active in the Taos and Santa Fe fur trade. At the well-known spring just above Boydsville, he had sponsored fur trapper rendezvous where trappers and traders periodically met to conduct their business.

Mr. Sublette died in 1845, years before the Denver & Rio Grande made its appearance, but his name was already associated with the area in a positive way, so Boydsville generally became known as Sublette, without much publicity or conscious thought. The old name was forgotten.

9

KISS OF DEATH

Sam Gonzales knew that a storm was coming. In confidence, he began to question his friend Eli about his intentions. Sam could see no good resulting from a confrontation between Leo Garcia and Eli Martinez. It would be bad publicity for the Denver & Rio Grande Western as both were valued employees, and it would be harmful in other ways, certainly for one of them. Sam could smell blood in the air.

On July 11, 1927, Eli was driving the Eastbound train. His position in the engineer's seat in the locomotive cab put him on the right side in clear sight of Arri's home when he eased the train to a stop, the tender underneath the waterspout.

He'd sounded his signature whistle, of course, and the coal bucket was in place, but Arri was missing. The conductor and the brakemen were at the rear of the train on the left side, looking at the undercarriage of a parlor car, the last car in the consist. Eli told Sam to go back and give them a hand. Sam gave him a knowing look, again almost saying no, Eli, don't do it, don't find her and talk to her. They'd passed the section gang with Leo Garcia in the lead about two miles to the west. Eli and Sam both knew, in essence, that the coast was clear.

Another coal shed encounter was possible, though not for sure. As Eli climbed down from the cab, he saw Arriana leave her house and walk towards the small building, bucket in hand. Was she saying that she alone would fill the bucket? Or was she saying that she'd like for him to come to the shed?

Love – his heart and not his head – decided for him. The thought of those magical eyes pulled him towards her like a magnet. He walked to the coal house as she disappeared inside.

Arri had been reading about decisive women. She also had a fresh black eye and new bruising on her face. Another fall. Oh sure. She wasn't happy with Leo Garcia either because he'd just forgotten her birthday, her 26th. And ignoring a woman's special day isn't very wise.

Arriana figured she knew what Clara Bow or Mae West would do.

She gathered up her courage as Eli entered the coal shed in the subdued light. The only illumination came from the open door. She said nothing but approached him and quickly and silently put her arms around his back and pulled him to her and kissed him. Hard and in a determined way as if she'd thought about this for weeks – which she had – and was determined not to lose her nerve.

Eli, though surprised, responded and kissed her back. His head went light. He felt her breasts against his chest through her dress. Her lips had the softness of velvet. He thought as the Los Mogotes volcano had done a few million years ago, he might erupt. His body responded immediately in a decisive way, a bit embarrassing, but it might have been more embarrassing if it had not, under the circumstances.

They held the kiss and embraced for a prolonged minute until both seemed to come to a place in their senses that said – this is crazy. They separated. Arri blushed, grabbed the bucket of coal, and walked away quickly towards the house. Eli peeked around the doorway of the shed and watched, her uneven walk just adding the frosted, sweet icing to the cake of his heart. Yes, Eli loved that woman, and never more than at that moment, and he knew he wanted her for his wife, for their lifetime!

Eli also knew that he had to stand in the coal shed for a couple of minutes and convince his body to behave itself so he could walk back to the locomotive. He went back when he could, glancing at the house for Arri, but she was nowhere in sight.

No matter. Eli now knew she felt the same way about him that he did about her. It was just a matter of getting it all sorted out. But what a thing and a lot of sorting had to take place.

Eli knew more. In their brief embrace, he saw the new black eye, saw the bruises on Arri's face. He had seen marks like those before, but they had been from a distance. Granted, she may have fallen inside the house, though anyone with good sense knew she'd have to be very uncoordinated to fall repeatedly. And Eli didn't believe her injuries were in any way related to her limp, any ability of hers to be steady on her feet inside her home.

Eli knew Leo Garcia had again harmed Arri. Leo, the war hero. Big, brave man. Hard-nosed section gang foreman. Once again, he'd beaten up the woman who lived with him in marriage and provided for his every need, including those in the bedroom.

Eli realized then he could kill the man who treated Arriana like that.

Sam Gonzales was his faithful friend. If Eli could confess his feelings to anyone, it was Sam. They left Sublette eastbound. Sam could quickly see that the locomotive wasn't the only thing steamed up. Eli Martinez was about to pop a valve. He wouldn't answer any of Sam's questions as to what was wrong, but Sam knew something dramatic had taken place. Had Arriana Garcia told Eli to forget it? Not likely when they passed the east station limit, and Leo sounded his now regular signature whistle – the first long being the AaaaaaaaaaahRiiiiiiiiiiiiiiiiiiii sound!

Eli turned to Sam, looked directly at him, and said: "Sam, I love that woman. If he hits her again and hurts her again, I'm going to kill him."

The intensity of what Eli said shocked Sam. It left little doubt in his mind that Eli Martinez meant just that.

10

SUBLETTE SECRETS

The cat was out of the bag, at least as between Eli and Sam. During subsequent days, Eli opened up about his feelings. Sam already knew, of course, that Eli had broken off his relationship with Maria Lopez. And when more than one person knows a thing, soon it's no longer a secret.

Others of the train crew, too, had noticed little things about the Sublette stops. People in tune with each other, as were Eli and Arriana, are often so much in tune that they overlook or ignore others who may be seeing things.

The suspected love saga of Eli and Arriana began to be the subject of backroom chatter, bunkhouse gossip. A whisper here, a suspicion voiced there. There had always been an uneasy, unspoken truce about the topic of Arriana Garcia and her beauty and her sour relationship with Leo Garcia that resulted in her being kicked around, beaten. Discussion of it was taboo because of Leo's meanness, his war hero status, his value as a critical foreman for the Denver & Rio Grande Western. But there's nothing that human beings seem to enjoy more than to see a big man fall.

Many began to wonder how this would all play out.

11

THE MODEL A PLAN

Whenever Eli had a few days off, he stayed at his house in Conejos. A friend, Jose Villela, had a Model T. It was old but ran well. Prohibition was in, had been in place since 1920, and would be until 1933, but there was always a place for those in the know to get a drink. Dance halls were popular, and liquor usually available at them. Gangsters country-wide made sure of that. Jose drove to Alamosa sometimes to dance and drink a beer, and Eli would go with him.

Eli had never been tempted to drink – *what was the purpose?* But having given up Maria for Arri and not having made much progress towards a relationship with Arriana that would pass the test of family and community, occasionally he would now have a few. Drowning his sorrows, Eliseo had heard it called. When he returned to his house, Jose dropping him off, he was alone and didn't have to worry about his folks or other family or friends knowing about it.

At any rate, Jose was the driver. If Eli had gotten in trouble over an accident or other incident and he'd been drunk, he might have lost his job with the railroad.

His troubles over Arri made him unhappy and were frustrating. He and Jose had been friends for years. Jose worked at a grocery store in Antonito owned by his uncle and lived in the railroad town just one mile from Conejos. Eli didn't want to confide his situation in Jose, but when one is sad over love, things slip out, and such was the case.

"What's wrong?" asked Jose, "you don't seem too happy. Dolores Baez wanted to dance, and you wouldn't give her the time of day. She's a nice girl, beautiful. What's going on?"

Eli hesitated then told Jose that he was okay, just a little tired from hard work. Jose didn't believe that but didn't push it.

Eli had another beer that made three he'd put away. His head was buzzing. "Damn!" he suddenly almost shouted.

He told Jose that yes, something was wrong. "Don't tell anybody, okay?" Eli spilled the beans to his friend. Jose knew both Arri's family and Leo's family and of Leo Garcia's status in the community. Jose was stunned, a little shocked. Immediately he knew this was a bad thing.

"What are you thinking?" he asked Eli.

"I think I'm in love for the first time. I want her, damn the consequences. I think she's in danger."

He told Jose of the injuries he'd seen, of Arri's mistreatment of which he was aware. Recently he'd seen her in Sublette on a Sunday when she dressed over and above her usual daily attire. It was a day off so far as possible for Arri – for example, the Sunday night meal was cornbread and milk, easily prepared compared to a more considerable amount and variety of food.

Arri had been wearing her unique built-up shoe, and she walked much better, though her limp mattered not in the least to Eli. Her uneven gait accentuated his desire to protect her. And Eli also thought that Arri might feel better if she walked more normally, more like others.

A week later, he saw her on another Sunday when he was driving the '89, pulling an eastbound freight, and he stopped for water at Sublette. Arri was again dressed more careful than usual but had her old shoes back on. She walked with her normal limp as he watched her go to the coal bunker. Eli saw Leo working on the siding in the yard nearby, so he knew it unwise to walk to the shed.

But Eliseo saw Willie Estrada over by the first bunk-house and knew, of course, of the unique way he was thought of by Arri and the others, possibly save Leo. So he made his way to Willie and asked him why Mrs. Garcia didn't have her good shoes on, the day being a Sunday.

Willie told him that her husband had made her put them away, that he didn't want her to wear them as they'd draw more attention from the workers.

Leo's jealousy resulted in Arri's punishment, Eli believed. She was forced to limp when she didn't have to when she could have been using her good shoes. And why couldn't she have more than one pair? Leo Garcia made enough money.

Eli was incensed!

He told Jose about what he'd seen and heard at Sublette. The more he talked about it, the madder he got. He had a fourth beer, one more than he'd ever consumed at one sitting. He was loaded, threw caution to the wind.

"Jose, Leo Garcia doesn't deserve that woman. If he continues to mistreat her, beat her, I'm going to kill him!"

Jose was shaken. Eliseo Martinez, his friend, would stand up for himself, he knew that, and nobody pushed him around, but he'd never been a violent person. Jose never expected to hear such talk from Eli. He figured it was best to change the conversation, tone things down. Jose decided to talk to Eli about cars.

Colorado/New Mexico Highway 17 was completed from Antonito to Chama in 1923. With more cars and trucks in use, things were beginning to change, even for the railroad.

In good weather, at least, people with motor vehicles or with friends who owned them were driving when they used to ride the train. Some farmers and ranchers were beginning to haul produce and cattle and sheep using trucks. And Ford had made a big announcement just this past May.

The Model T had been discontinued after many years. Ford would dedicate all their factory production to a new Model A with seven different body styles. It would come in four colors and would range in price from $500 to $1200. The Model A would have a safety glass windshield, 4-wheel brakes, and hydraulic shock absorbers. It would be their first model to feature the Ford blue oval logo, which would become a company icon. The model change quickly proved to be a big success. Over 400,000 Model A's were sold in the first two weeks after its debut.

Jose reminded Eli that he was now a prosperous young man who had money and a good future and could afford to make the payments on a new Ford. He would be the talk of the community if he went to Denver, got one, and drove it back.

Eli had already been thinking about getting a Model T, so this Model A plan appealed to him. Now and then, Arri came back to the San Luis Valley for some special occasion, like a family wedding or funeral, and Eli thought how she'd be impressed to see him in a new Ford. Maybe that would speed up her thinking process so that they might get something done in their relationship.

"Hey, I might do that, Jose. Want to go up to Denver with me soon, and we'll look at the Model A's? I get passes to ride the train so that it won't cost us anything. We can drive the car back if I get one. That'll be a great trip!" Denver was easily reachable from Antonito, 280 rail miles to the north, and the idea was feasible. There was already a quality road over that distance for a return trip.

Eli's attention temporarily left the Arri and Leo saga, and Jose was glad. He drove Eli home from Alamosa and saw him safely to bed before going to his own house.

Ford talk aside, though, Jose couldn't forget what he'd heard Eli say.

"I'm going to kill him!" Holy cow. Jose was suddenly glad he didn't have a serious involvement, especially with a married woman.

Jose went to sleep very late that night. He was worried about what Eli had told him and wished he hadn't heard it.

12

TRAINS AND PLANES

Trains were the engine of American transportation and commerce for 100 years, roughly 1850 through 1950. But in 1927, Eli, like many others, was considering getting himself a motor car. Up until now, had Eli wanted to go to Alamosa or farther north, without a doubt he'd have taken the train. He could ride it anytime free as a railroad engineer, a significant benefit of employment.

Once at his train stop, though, he'd have to walk to his destination if he didn't hire a wagon or horse. With a Ford, he could drive straight there.

Many people were thinking the same way. It wouldn't have an immediate effect on train travel, but it would later.

Airplanes were out and about and becoming refined, more than a novelty. During World War I, they had become an essential part of both enemy and allied military might. At first, they scouted and observed. But seeing them overhead, soldiers on both sides shot at them, of course. They were the enemy. Some were shot down. Some were set afire. The pilots wore no parachutes, and the predictable result, of course, was a disaster for the flier.

The development of crude bombs took place. Machine guns appeared on aircraft. Pilots began an earnest effort to destroy each other, and many did. Airplanes didn't play a decisive role in the conflict, but they played an increasingly important part.

After the war, military airplanes sold as surplus for a few hundred dollars. Ex-military pilots and others traveled the country, barnstorming, performing air shows, giving rides. Americans increasingly became familiar with flying machines.

Initially, they were a novelty, but then they began to encroach on things which were the province of trains.

Railroads like the Denver & Rio Grande Western had RPOs, Railroad Post Office cars. Mail contracts were a lucrative part of their business. Aircraft in many places became better suited to carry the mail. Its weight was often within the limits that planes could transport. At perhaps 100 mph, delivery was faster, though that might not be true in mountain country where the level ground on which to land was scarce. Bad weather was still a significant limiting factor, much more so than it was for trains, and places like the San Juan Mountains had unpredictable conditions.

But rudimentary airlines began to pop up and siphon off railroad passenger traffic. Of course, there were accidents, but there were train accidents, too. People began to be obsessed with the idea of air travel.

In 1927, though, severe inroads into train commerce in both passenger traffic and freight were yet to come. And few people believed it could or would happen.

Then something took place that made people start to seriously consider the possibilities surrounding air travel. Charles Lindbergh took off from Roosevelt Airfield, Long Island, New York, just before 7 am on May 20, 1927. After 33 hours and 29 minutes, he landed at le Bourget Aerodrome, Paris, France. It was the first solo transatlantic flight. Lindbergh won a $25,000 prize. His airplane, The Spirit of St. Louis, had been built by Ryan Aeronautical Company, especially for the flight attempt.

One in every two pilots who previously tried crossing the Atlantic died during the attempt. Six aviators had lost their lives in the previous six tries to win the huge prize. Lindbergh returned as a hero, treated to a ticker-tape parade in New York City on his arrival from France by ocean liner. Now people seriously considered the beginnings of air travel.

Charles Lindbergh had dramatically demonstrated a vision of the future.

But for the time being, the present and near term remained bright for professional trainmen like Eli Martinez and Samuel Gonzales.

13

HAULER OF THE MAULER

Eli and fireman Larry Montegon took a trainload of perlite from south of Antonito to Alamosa, driving engine # 484. Perlite is a rocklike substance with air bubbles in it. It will float in water. Ground up, it's used as a substitute for sand in cement and is a money product of the San Luis Valley. The plant that processes it is just below Antonito.

Fireman Montegon was privy to some locker room gossip about engineer Martinez, concerning Eli's interest in the Sublette section foreman's wife. People were talking a little, though quietly. So Larry Montegon was curious but wary of broaching the subject right away since he didn't pair up with Eli too often.

The perlite gondolas were dropped in the Alamosa yard for later shipment north. Eli and Larry were to run light back to Antonito but received new train orders at the last minute. They were directed to pull, and then drop off, a first-class parlor car on the Romeo siding, six miles north of Antonito, just three miles from Manassa, Colorado.

A bit of mystery surrounded the car. That type was nearly always reserved for a Very Important Person. The engineer and fireman wondered who might be inside. A concern, of course, was that it could be an executive of the railroad, which meant that any small mistake on their part could result in criticism, so they were on high alert.

Eli, who of late had thought of little beyond Arri Garcia, even had her pushed into a backchannel of his head. A rare thing for him.

At Alamosa, they watched as a well-built man in a suit, surrounded by others who seemed to be catering to his every move, walked to the parlor car. Who was that? He looked familiar. Oh, my goodness! Both recognized him at the same time. It was the Manassa Mauler!

William Harrison "Jack" Dempsey, heavyweight champion of the world from 1919 to 1926, had grown up in Manassa, just nine miles northeast of Antonito. Kid Blackie was another of his nicknames. His punching power and aggressive fighting style had made him one of the most famous boxers in history. His fights set attendance and financial records, including the first million-dollar gate.

Jack Dempsey lost the heavyweight title in September 1926 to Gene Tunney, but his popularity in southern Colorado remained at an all-time high. Local boy, the Manassa Mauler, makes good!

Neither Eli nor Larry Montegon was an autograph seeker. The thought didn't occur to either one to ask for his signature, but they sure wanted to meet him. Of course, high-ranking Denver & Rio Grande Western officials were in the group surrounding Dempsey. So

Eli and Larry professionally went about their duties. They backed the '84 up carefully. The brakemen had finished their workday and gotten off the perlite freight in Alamosa, so Larry dismounted and oversaw the coupling, done smoothly.

Somehow pleasing the heavyweight champion, well, okay, ex-heavyweight champion, was more important than worrying about the officials on board. Eli got the signal to depart, sounded the whistle two long bursts, and smoothly pushed the throttle forward, getting engine # 484 headed quickly down the straight track to the Romeo siding.

Pulling off the siding and coming to a smooth stop, fireman Montegon again left the cab and uncoupled the car, to be left in place presumably for Mr. Dempsey's return to points north. Two luxurious black Packard automobiles were waiting nearby.

Eli and Larry waited for a signal from one of the executives that it was okay to move out to Antonito. None was immediately forthcoming. The crowd surrounding the Champ and including him walked to the locomotive. Jack Dempsey, an outgoing man and very fit, bounded up the ladder to the '84's cab.

"Just wanted to tell you boys that had to be the best train ride I've ever taken!" said Dempsey, shaking, in turn, Eli's then Larry's hand. "Thanks for the good work! Hope you're driving on the way back."

Larry and Eli were temporarily speechless. Those words coming from the heavyweight champion of the world, who undoubtedly traveled on many trains, were quite the compliment, and in front of the company's big boys! It was hard to believe they'd shaken a hand that was so famous.

"Why are you here, sir?" blurted out Larry, never a shy one.

"The local folks want to set up a museum honoring me, and I've come to discuss details. And it's just good to get back home for a while. Manassa is a nice quiet place compared to where I usually am, and sometimes I get tired of the noise and confusion. So it's good to be here. You fellows be safe, and thanks for the great ride. Hope to see you again!"

With that, he backed down the ladder and was gone, surrounded by the noise and confusion, it seemed, that he said he wanted to avoid. Both Eli and Larry wondered how much rest he'd get in Manassa, Colorado. But it was great to see him, and be complimented personally by the Champ!

Eli pulled out of the siding onto the main track, headed south. He and Larry were still slightly overwhelmed. Jack Dempsey! It took reaching the next road crossing for Eli to get his head back on straight. A warning whistle of two longs – one short – one long was required. Eli thought how proud Arri would have been to share this moment.

He had a quick vision of the Manassa Mauler beating the snot out of Leo Garcia, seeing how Leo, the tough guy, would like that.

AaaaaaaaaaaahRiiiiiiiiiiiiiiiiiiiiii! went the first note.

Well, that was a little unusual from what I remember of Eli's signature, thought Larry, but he said nothing out loud.

14

JUST A QUICK COLD ONE

Back at the Antonito yard, Eli eased the '84 into the engine shed. It was due for servicing. Typically he and Larry would have made a go-around of the locomotive, doing some routine oiling and a visual inspection, but that wasn't required today. The roundhouse crew would take care of it.

"Wow, a great day, Eli. Want to get a cold one? Losario's dance hall is open. What say you to just one? My treat," said Larry.

Eli had begun again to think of Arri, and relaxing while drinking a cold beer seemed an excellent way to continue that. He and Larry weren't close friends, but why not? So they went to Losario's.

They drank quietly, making small talk, discussing how great it had been to see the champ, Jack Dempsey. Manassa, Colorado, had done well for itself, having him for a native son. They wondered about their chances of pulling him back to Alamosa but knew it was unlikely. They'd been on a particular freight run, a one-time thing, and had just been in the right place at the right time. Indeed, it wasn't to be.

As they talked, Larry tried to coax Eli into having a few more beers, loosen him up, and see if he'd speak about Sublette. Eli had just one, was tired, ready to go home, and did. No such discussion took place. But when Sublette was mentioned once by Larry, Eli gave him a funny look. Larry asked him about his whistle signature sound he'd heard earlier, something new. But Eli was non-committal.

"Never too old to try something different, Larry," said Eli, giving him a wink. "Never know what's going to happen in this old world, do we?"

Larry and Eli parted, Larry still curious, but asking no more.

15

RADIO NEWS

Eli awoke early the next morning, another day off before he was scheduled to take out the westbound New Mexico Express. Sam Gonzales was again set to be his fireman. He couldn't wait to tell Sam about meeting the Champ. He hoped to see Arri for a moment at Sublette and tell her, too. She'd be very excited. So far as Eli knew, there'd been no advance publicity about the Manassa Mauler being back in his hometown.

He did some chores around his house, finding that staying busy kept him from always thinking about Arriana, although it wasn't much of a relief. She dominated his day.

Eli, my boy, he thought to himself, *you've got to get this sorted out.*

He went to his folks' home that night. Maybe he'd hear some news of Jack Dempsey's visit on the radio. Eli marveled at how things had changed for not only his mother and father but for other people in Conejos and Antonito recently.

Radio was coming in a big way and kept them up

to date on what was happening in the world, a rapidly changing world it seemed if events of 1927 were any measure.

Eli was making a good living and had only himself to support, though he would like to change that, at least with the woman for whom he cared. He could afford to help his parents with new things to make their lives easier, even more entertaining.

The Columbia Phonographic Broadcasting System was formed earlier in the year and had gone on air with 47 stations. One was in Denver, and on good weather nights, Conejos listeners heard it. Only four other local families had been able to afford a radio, all of them courtesy of having railroad workers with a decent income during these good times.

Eli had helped his folks get one. It had cost $74.95, a lot of money. To save their pride, Eli wouldn't tell them how much it had set him back but said if they'd pay five dollars, even that amount not affordable for them to have extra, he'd provide the rest.

The Martinez family, it seemed, was suddenly more popular in their neighborhood. Friends dropped by and asked to listen to the latest in news and entertainment. Like birds on a wire, they lined up in the living room, sitting on the couch, first come first seated. Mrs. Martinez soon tired of the invasion of her home, and her husband took the radio to the front porch, and neighbors were asked to bring their chairs. They gladly did, and often women coming by with their families brought food.

Electricity was then available in southern Colorado, so running an extension cord onto the porch for the radio was no problem.

As a group, the Conejos news junkies heard these things on the radio during 1927:

The first transatlantic telephone call was made from New York City to London, England. Imagine a telephone line under the ocean, all the way across the Atlantic!

Listeners heard that the Flatheads Gang had robbed an armored car near Pittsburg, Pennsylvania, the first such robbery. Crime was running rampant!

Learned the worst national disaster in United States history had taken place during April and May when the Great Mississippi River Flood occurred, affecting 700,000 people. Hundreds drowned.

Buck v. Bell was decided in the Supreme Court of the United States, permitting compulsory sterilization of people with intellectual disabilities.

Bombings in Bath Township, Michigan, resulted in 45 deaths, mostly children. It was called the Bath School Disaster.

Of course, the news that Charles Lindbergh had made the first non-stop solo trans-Atlantic flight from New York to Paris in a single-seat plane called the Spirit of St. Louis was a big deal. How would airplanes affect trains, wondered some Conejos listeners? They didn't think it would be very much or very soon.

In May 1927, the first live demonstration of television came from the Bell Telephone Building in New York City. According to the radio in Conejos, 600 members of the American Institute of Electrical Engineers had seen it. What was television? Do you mean that live moving pictures of real people could be seen? That was almost beyond the belief of Colorado listeners, something for the future a long time down the road.

President Calvin Coolidge made use of the radio, and his inauguration was the first presidential broadcast on that medium. He used radio to announce he would not seek reelection.

"I do not choose to run for President in 1927," Silent Cal, silent no more, said, and they heard him say it.

A very few Conejos residents had seen a silent movie. There was a movie theatre in Alamosa. Now a talking motion picture- the first - called *The Jazz Singer*, starring Al Jolson, was out and had become an enormous success. It was advertised on the radio. Conejos listeners wondered how long it would take for that movie to get to Colorado? They also were curious to know if they'd have the extra 10 cents it cost for a ticket whenever it finally did.

Baseball was very popular in the United States. Colorado was no exception. Southern Colorado radio listeners, if the weather was good and permitted reception, heard some live broadcasts of the four-game sweep of the Pittsburg Pirates by the New York Yankees – Murderer's Row – in the World Series.

Murderer's Row was the Yankees' fearsome lineup of power hitters that included Babe Ruth, Lou Gehrig, Tony Lazzeri, and Bob Meusel. You couldn't stop those Yankees!

Yankee player Babe Ruth was the most famous athlete of America in 1927, and everyone wanted to hear about him and his high style of living. He was known as the Sultan of Swat or The Bambino and was the greatest gate attraction in baseball all through the 1920s. In 1927, he hit 60 home runs, a new single-season record! Radio brought all this directly to listeners' homes.

And of course, hearing the news from Ford Motor

Company that after 15 million, the Model T would cease production. Their new car would be the Model A, with many improvements. When announced, they shook their heads in awe. Who in the world in Conejos, Colorado, they wondered, would be the first owner of a new Model A? Just seeing one driving through town would be quite the thing.

Eli smiled to himself when he heard that. Maybe it'll be me, he thought, and won't my friends and neighbors be surprised!

And yes, there had been mention of Jack Dempsey's visit to his hometown, Manassa, Colorado. The radio station had probably been tipped off by Denver & Rio Grande Western officials, who wanted the publicity. When Conejos residents learned that their native son, Eliseo Martinez, had been the engineer on the Manassa Mauler's train, they were ecstatic.

Look who rode our train! Look who drove him!

Things were good in Conejos, Colorado, as life forged ahead, with little hint as to the coming storm.

16

MIND THE TORPEDOES

Eli and Sam were early to work the following day, their habit. "The early bird gets the apple," Eli's dad had always told him. Eli thought it was supposed to be the worm but wouldn't contradict his father. At any rate, Eliseo Martinez liked apples and especially the kind that came to good employees, and he'd never been late, though he'd been close once or twice due to unforeseen circumstances.

A hotshot freight, all the way through to Chama, the division point, was assigned to Eli and Sam. They'd be pulling it with # 483, just coming out of maintenance at the Antonito shop. Of all things, the most significant part of their consist was several flatcars of brand new, just off the production line, Model T cars and trucks. Just off an assembly line now closed to any more Model T's, per the information put out by Ford and confirmed by the Martinez family radio.

Eli guessed that dealers in places like Durango and Farmington were getting a special price on the close-out stock and were taking advantage. The Model A's wouldn't hit area dealerships for a while yet.

But there was something Eli didn't like. They were to continue straight through Sublette without watering, to stop at Toltec station instead. Another freight was eastbound, and they'd need to get to the Toltec siding to let it pass. Scheduling on a single-line track with both eastbound and westbound traffic was always a challenge.

Along the side of the track, put in place during the initial construction of the line, was a telegraph wire. If a train had problems, a trained telegrapher on board had to report the issue to the Alamosa dispatcher, so that schedule adjustments were assured. For safety's sake, of course.

Well, that's the way it had been until 1925 when the telegraph was augmented with telephone handsets using the same wires. Now it was easy for any of the train crew to notify dispatch since not everyone had to know Morse Code.

There were other actions to take during a train breakdown or failure to follow train orders. If another train was following yours, or another was approaching you from the front, a brakeman hot-footed it out a mile or more and waved a warning lantern with red lights – lit red flares called 'fusees' which lasted from 20 to 30 minutes each – and set torpedoes on the track.

Torpedoes were explosive charges which were strapped across the rails so the locomotive wheels would set them off. They caused no damage to the track or locomotive but made a terrific noise. Hearing one or more, an engineer knew to shut his train down, trouble ahead.

Engineer Martinez, fireman Gonzales, and the other train crew – the conductor and two brakemen - left Antonito on time. Eli was disappointed, to say the least, to know they wouldn't stop in Sublette, where he might get a brief chance to greet Arri.

They worked their way up the average 1% grade to Lava Tank. Climbing west, the steepest gradient of the track didn't exceed 1.42% up to Cumbres Pass, the high point on the line at 10,015 feet. That was much easier to climb than the eastbound 4% grade from Chama up to Cumbres. In places, the westbound grade was down to less than a foot per 100 feet forward. An easy climb for # 483, a real workhorse.

Passing Lava Tank, Eli sounded the whistle so that Alvie Johnson, the pump operator in his shack over by the Rio de Los Pinos, would hear them. Eli was required to make that report. Alvie was surprised the first time he'd listened to a new signature whistle but soon learned it was that of Eli Martinez. He didn't know why Eli had changed his tune, but knew him as a straight-shooter with good sense and figured there must be a logical reason. So be it.

Eli and Sam continued to drive their freight uphill. Eli loved the upside-down ice cream cone shape of San Antonio Peak, which as usual, was on their left. He knew a little of its history, was aware that Native Americans of long ago had gotten their obsidian for arrow and spear points from San Antonio Peak. Eliseo had heard it still had an active vent top dead center, but geologists, people who knew about such things, said a few million years had passed since it last popped its cork. How they knew that Eli had no clue, but he trusted they were right.

From time to time, geologists rode the Denver & Rio Grande Western into these mountains to conduct such studies and learn more about the area.

Just on the right, the twin peaks of Los Mogotes volcano, also long dead, came into sight. Eli remembered that Colorado Highway 17 ran along its southern flank. The Colorado state highway department finished the gravel highway in 1923, and Martinez had been over it twice in a motor vehicle. Eli was amazed it was possible to get to Chama that way almost as fast now as on the train; if the weather was good, the road not too muddy or covered with snow and ice. And if there had not been too many flat tires on the car or truck he rode in. Sometimes the thought of that made him nervous as motor vehicles began to haul things like produce. But Eli didn't see how they could ever compete with the train.

Big Horn section house came along next. He entered the first leg of the Three Ply, where he could see the three levels of track.

Near the tail end of the first short straightway of the Three Ply, two small children played in a swing. Some cables hung from the strongest limb of a big ponderosa pine. The swing was one of their very few toys. But Eli knew that when the youngsters were big enough, they'd be helping their father and mother with chores around their home. And their folks could use the help. There was a lot to do. Life wasn't easy, and the whole family's assistance was often needed.

The section house was on Eli's right as he rounded the first curve to enter the second leg of the Three Ply. Earlier in the railroad's history, there'd been a hotel at this location, but the advent of larger and faster locomotives overcame the need for a place for passengers to lodge. The Denver & Rio Grande Western, always eager to save a buck when a building was needed somewhere else, had torn it down to reuse the materials several years before Eli began his career. He would like to have seen it, to have eaten a good trout meal there, which had been the special fare. Local fishermen had caught fish daily from the Rio de Los Pinos just over the hills to the south and sold them to the cook.

Those were the days of old, but it was now 1927. Eli continued into Whiplash Curve. Westbound on the top leg of the Three Ply, he soon saw on the right the familiar rock carving of the thunderbird. He knew there were more such carvings on that same hillside, but the thunderbird was the only one visible from the track.

Eli made a mental note –hike up there someday soon and take a look. Wouldn't it be great to take Arri there on a picnic? They could ride the train – the engineer would make a special quick stop for them – they could spend the day – and catch the Express on the way back, or even a freight.

Eli caught himself daydreaming and had to remember that Arri might have trouble with such a climb, with her crippled leg. But he could help her get up there. *Uh oh, mind drifting again – better get my head straight,* he thought to himself, *got a train to run here!*

Eliseo Martinez knew that men had been hurt, even killed, because their eyes and minds were turned inward toward some yearning wish like this. In spite of his wanting to think of Arri, he had to concentrate on the job at hand.

He was smart enough to know that while he could run his locomotive proficiently, one had to keep one's mind focused. You needed to have other train crew who paid attention as well. The saying was out there: "You can't stop a moving train." Well, Eli knew you could, but not quickly. The train is cumbersome; its momentum a serious thing. The railroad company talked about safe travel to The Public. But the truth was a steam locomotive is a controlled explosion rolling down the track. The pressure inside the boiler is 195 to 200 pounds per square inch, depending on the model of engine you are driving. Danger is ever-present. Water is critical. The fireman has to watch the water level in the boiler, which changes as the engine heads up or down a grade since water will naturally stay level while the level of the boiler tilts. The engineer and fireman have to remain focused, work as a team.

The train is a massive collection of steel parts, synchronized to work together perfectly, racing along on slick tracks made of more steel, steel wheels on those steel tracks. Only a few inches of contact – steel to steel – hold things in place. Mistake-free performance is required of men who, since they are humans, make human mistakes. Perfection is needed that doesn't exist. No one tells The Public this. The truth is, luck is critical, and every train may run out of it.

Some of the crew have been in accidents, during which they spun out of control, and hoping to avoid tragedy again, they look to the rear, not forward. They work in the baggage car or other parts of the consist. They've seen people meet their death trying to save a few seconds by racing the train across an intersection, ignoring warning signals. They've even seen fuel trucks gambling with the lives of their occupants.

But with anything so massive, with so much momentum, no real safety exists elsewhere on the train. A wheel slipping off the track, a mismanaged boiler that explodes, the ramming together of cars when the engine impacts something – sometimes just luck saves crewmen from injury or death, no matter their position on board. Passengers are subject to the same risks, though no one will tell them that ahead of time. Sometimes they just have to be lucky too.

All the rules are there for a reason. They have to be obeyed. The locomotive whistles all have a meaning, listen carefully. Don't stand between the rails. Is your equipment working correctly? Does your lantern have oil in it? Don't blind someone with its light. Don't put a load like oil field pipe on an open flatcar where it will be dangerous next to a car such as a caboose with people in it, in case of collision. Don't leave a knuckle closed at the head end of a car. Face ahead when jumping off the train. Grab solid hold of a handhold at every opportunity.

Switches are dangerous, and it's critical to be sure they are set correctly. Check twice, then recheck. Don't be hesitant, make up your mind, and do a thing. It's always better to be where the engineer can see you. Don't wear rings which can become entangled with equipment. The train is not forgiving when you forget. Pass signals on the way you receive them.

Don't hunker down or even stand between cars, watch out, increase your attention when in that position. Strain your ears for the rollout. Don't daydream about your girlfriend, your wife. The massive wheels are unforgiving, and your body is no match. A dry rail is slick, a wet track even more so, the danger is always close at hand.

Always make sure your Hamilton pocket watch is set correctly. If you don't have a good watch, buy one. Time is critical for trains; even a few seconds can make the difference between a good run and disaster. Lives may be lost or forever changed by small ticks of the clock. Take your time hacks seriously.

Read train orders carefully, more so in the dark. Trust your fellow trainmen, but adjust quickly if that trust is misplaced. People are tired, hungry, and their attention may wander. Men have died because they or someone else was distracted. The cemeteries are full of such men. Be careful, and be lucky if you weren't.

Pay attention.

Remember that when a man loses his life on the railroad, he was working a job he probably loved and was with friends who felt the same way when he died.

Eli ran these things through his mind and did his best to focus. Soon he passed the Big Horn wye on the left. It was there mainly for snow removal trains to turn around, so they didn't have to go all the way to Lava Tank or even Antonito. Big Horn siding was on the right, as was another telephone booth. Eli knew that here was a bell hooked to the telephone line so that a train in either direction rang it in Alamosa dispatch. The dispatcher thus knew a train had passed this location, and that should coincide with the train schedule. If not, something was off and had to be corrected. It was the only such signal on the entire 64 miles between Antonito and Chama.

Sublette wasn't too far now. Again Eli regretted not being able to come to a stop.

Slowing at the station warning sign, Eli sounded the whistle, made that first long note say AaaaaaaaaaaahRiiiiiiiiiiiiiiiiiiiii! If he couldn't come to a halt, at least he would let someone know he was thinking of her. Passing through the east end of the station, he saw Leo Garcia and six of the section hands working on the track, within sight of the section house.

Sam glanced at Eli with a relieved look. Both knew that Sam was thinking that maybe God was looking out for Eli today. Had the train stopped, and Eli approached Arri, and Leo saw, well, who knew what might have happened?

As they went through Sublette at slow speed, Eli saw Arri walking from her house to the coal shed, bucket in hand. She had her characteristic limp, also her inherent beauty, though dressed in everyday working clothes. Goodness, thought Eli, glancing her way, she can't look bad no matter what.

Arri glanced at # 483's cab as it went by, caught Eli's eye for a brief moment, but otherwise gave no hint of recognition or greeting.

Eli knew that by doing so, however, she was thinking of him, and that would make the rest of this trip more manageable.

Sam glanced at Eli and knew that Eli knew that Arri was thinking of him, and that would make the rest of the trip easier for Eli.

What a world they lived in, Sam thought! *What did love do to people?* One day he had to give it a try.

Maybe I'd try it, he considered further, *if it weren't as dangerous as this looked to be.*

Engine # 483 tugged away at the freight, the Model T's collectively going as fast on the flatcars as they might have been traveling individually on Highway 17. Perhaps more quickly.

They arrived at Toltec station on time, pulled onto the siding. Eli had given his new signature whistle. Was there some chance that Arri might have heard it back in Sublette? The sound did bounce up and down the canyons. He imagined that she'd listened to the whistle and hoped it put a smile on her face.

A face he hoped wasn't marred at present with another black eye or another injury. *Must not think about that,* Eli mused.

The eastbound train raced by on the main line, scant inches away.

Then they pressed on. Eli thought back five years when engine # 169, at the head of the New Mexico Express, was hit near this location by an eastbound locomotive running light, whose engineer thought he had more time to get to the Sublette siding. The wreck killed the engineer and fireman on the passenger train.

Then through the volcanic spires of Phantom Curve. Eli and Sam remembered long tiring nights when they'd seen strange shapes in the headlight, heard the wheels squealing in the curve of the track, almost believed the old trainmen's stories about these rails being haunted.

Did the apparitions of men who'd died beneath the massive wheels through carelessness or impatience live here? Were there ghosts who'd driven around a curve too fast? After working for hours on end, through blizzards and thunderstorms and hail, over thousands of miles, they were gone. Or were they? Trainmen often became philosophical at Phantom Curve.

Calico Cut, with those beautiful colored minerals in the rock, went by slowly. Here the roadbed was soft, the ground often muddy, and caution always mandatory.

Mud Tunnel came up, the trainmen hoping their locomotive's sparks didn't set the support timbers inside on fire as had happened in the past.

In three more miles, they slipped through Rock Tunnel, the deep drop-off into Toltec Gorge on their immediate left after clearing the tunnel, then the Garfield monument on the left too. *What an unusual location for a marker like that*, thought Eli, though he and the others had passed it so often they didn't dwell on it now.

He knew the story. The railroad had opened fully for business to Chama from Antonito in January of 1881. President James A. Garfield was shot in the Washington, DC, train station on July 2, 1881, just a scant five months later. The assassin, Charles Guiteau, was a political enemy of the president. President Garfield lingered until September 19th, when he died. The funeral service in his hometown of Cleveland, Ohio, was held a week later on September 26, 1881. The eastbound Colorado Express left Osier that day, its riders aware of the significance of the date – it was President Garfield's day to be honored.

The train crew vowed to do just that, at the most spectacular point of their trip, by the 600-foot drop-off just outside the west portal of Rock Tunnel.

The crew had stopped the train and held an impromptu memorial service to honor the president, who died in service of his country. Later the monument was erected by the Association of Ticket Agents and Freight Agents, the only such tribute to President Garfield in the United States.

A strange place perhaps, this remote area of the San Juan Mountains, but President Garfield had been president here too, and here it was and would stay.

Eli always noticed that the land changed in nature not far ahead, from the jagged mountains formed from volcanoes to what the experts said was sculpted by icebergs during the Ice Age. The valleys ahead, for the most part, had a smooth, rounded shape. The Ice Age began about three million years ago and lasted until around 11,000 years ago.

Icebergs from the tops of these mountain peaks slowly moved down by gravity and carved out the smoothly shaped valleys as they melted. At choke points called terminal moraines, they either met other icebergs with the two stopping each other where they dissolved in place; or they encountered terrain that was not favorable to their movement and stayed there. The latter was the case at Toltec Gorge, where the hard granite canyon was very narrow and wouldn't permit an iceberg to progress farther eastward.

Eli Martinez was a railroad engineer and loved his job, but when he thought about how land evolved, he found it fascinating and believed that in another life, with an opportunity to get the right education, he might have been interested in studying such things.

But today, his job was to get this freight to Chama, New Mexico, and the study of geology wasn't going to happen. He was simply on another path; others would have to do such work.

The train rumbled into Osier. He stayed to the right. There was a house track to his left, a siding that allowed another train to park in front of the section house and depot. The house track was empty. Since Eli had watered at Toltec, he drove on through, past the 50,000-gallon water tank on his left. There was a large coal platform also on his left, next to the tank and bunkhouse. Two section gang members were working near the coal platform and waved at the passing train.

Eli, of course, sounded his new whistle, which was now becoming known as his signature sound. Eli thought of you-know-who as he heard it bounce off Osier Mountain, to his right rear.

He moved over Cascade Creek on its high trestle, 137 feet above the watercourse. It was the highest point on the trip for the train over land. If he'd had a helper engine in front, it would have unhooked, gone across, and the train would have reconnected once both locomotives were clear. The German-designed steel bent trestle was sturdy, but it had always been railroad policy not to test it with the combined weight of two engines and tenders. Safety first!

Soon he and Sam were passing some bristlecone pines, about 100 of them along both sides of the roadbed. The bristlecones weren't typically found in this area of the Southern Rockies. They usually grew farther north. No one seemed to know why they were here, but railroaders learned this variety of pine tree could date back to the days of Jesus Christ, that they could live to be 2,000 years old or older. Some bristlecones that grew in the redwood forests of northern California were said to be almost 5,000 years old. *More mysteries of the universe* thought Eli briefly, but his present duties of throttling up, braking, stretching the train out smoothly, bunching it up without jerking when braking or slowing down, demanded his full attention, and that it got.

Now Los Pinos Valley was in sight. It was the hardest place in winter to keep the line open. It was a giant bowl, and weather swept down from all sides. In wintertime, snow often drifted 20 to 30 feet high.

OM, the rotary snowplow known as Old Maude, had been made in 1889. In 1923, the year Eli started with the company, another snow removal car, OY, had been added. OY had no such nickname. In winter, engineer Martinez was sometimes a driver of one of the up to seven locomotives that pushed OM or OY through these Los Pinos drifts. Or one of the trainmen who tried to. Sometimes the crews couldn't keep the trains rolling, and delays were the result. Eli thought about those winter days as he brushed past the Los Pinos water tank on his right. With sincere thankfulness, he glanced at the small coal warming shed next to the tank. He remembered bitterly cold days when that little building, all heated with coal, had been a welcome refuge.

He wound around and around and up towards Cumbres Pass, almost there. Through Tanglefoot Curve as some called it, the Balloon or Cumbres Loop according to others.

Eli and Sam had often smiled at the way Tanglefoot Curve had gotten its name. The upper track was 25 feet taller than the other one, just 75 feet away. In the early days, a brakeman on an eastbound had jumped from his long train, just assembled after being brought up in cuts from Chama to Cumbres. The practice was for a brakeman to scramble down the steep hill, over that 75-foot distance, crouch down near the rails, and check for hotboxes as his train rumbled past, then hop aboard the last car, his task completed. But on that occasion, the brakeman's feet tangled in some briers, and he almost fell into the path of his train. What a way to get a curve named for you!

Eli and Sam drifted into Cumbres Pass past the depot, slowing for another water stop near the section house, the last structure before heading down the steep 4% grade. Stopping under the water spout, they took on that precious liquid, something a steam engine by its very design and function had to have. The '83, like the other 480 series engines, carried nine and one-half tons of coal, more than enough for the 64 miles between Antonito and Chama, but its 5,000 gallons of water weren't sufficient to make the trip non-stop.

Meanwhile, the car inspector came from his home on their right, from his front door. Eli and Sam remembered snowy winter days when the inspector exited his house from the second-floor window. His job was to check the brakes on both westbound and eastbound trains. Cumbres was the high point on the railroad at 10,015 feet, and a train leaving either direction would be traveling downhill. Of course, the steep westbound grade demanded the most critical attention, as a failure to stop a train headed that way would most likely have fatal consequences. It was entirely appropriate to use the utmost caution on this next 12 miles into Chama. But it didn't unnecessarily scare either Eli or Sam who traveled it often. They had confidence in their braking system. According to legions of trainmen, if they were afraid, that was one thing, but they couldn't be cowards.

A young man named George Westinghouse had

invented air brakes for trains in 1870. In 1872 the Denver & Rio Grande was the first freight system in America to install them. So this railroad had more experience with air brakes than any other line.

Straight air brakes, where air pressure forced the brake shoes against the metal surface of the wheels, were later changed to a system where the air pressure forces the brake shoes away from the surface of the wheels. In the improved method, if pressure, typically about 80 pounds, failed – it was carried in a hose hooked together between all the cars – the brakes then closed in an 'emergency stop.' The train was brought safely to a halt and repairs made.

That had happened to both Eli and Sam several times, and they knew how to deal with it.

After the brakes were checked and partly retarded with the hand braking system so they'd drag just a little, and the tender was filled with water, Eli calmly said to Sam: "Here we go." Two bursts of the whistle signaled their start. Now Eli moved towards Chama, respectful of the descent they would make, but secure and confident in his and Sam's and the brakemen's ability to get them and their load there safely.

Eli glanced skyward and said a trainman's prayer picked up from others that covered the occasion and more: "Thank you, God, for Westinghouse brakes, safety couplers, and electric headlights!"

Cumbres Pass was left behind.

17

DOWN THE HILL

Down the 4% grade they went. You had to keep your eye on things and be alert at all times. Watch the steam, watch the air, and watch the water level in the boiler. Since the front of the locomotive tipped down, was lower than the cab, the water gauge would register low. But you didn't want the water level too high, either. Correctly injecting water into the boiler from the tender was important. It was just one of the many vital things.

One important thing was to keep your mind in gear, not to daydream. Pay attention. Eli needed to minimize his thoughts about Arriana Garcia on this section of track, 12 miles.

He and Sam continued their descent.

Going down the hill, anywhere really, you needed other trainmen you could trust to do their jobs well. One was aboard today, working as the head-end brakeman. His name was Red Griffin. He was a prankster, a man who liked to be funny or whatever his version of that was.

The human race produced many different personalities, and sure enough, some of them were jerks. A few of those found employment on the Denver & Rio Grande Western, and sooner or later, every crew ended up with at least one.The other category of man that everyone had their fair share of was the prankster or jokester, like Red Griffin. He worked with Eli and Sam quite often.

Both Eli and Sam had a sense of humor, but the locomotive cab was a place where you shouldn't be distracted. When in the front, Red clambered over the tender and locomotive doing his job, switching them onto sidings, performing other brakeman duties, and he was among the best, so was upfront often.

Red Griffin was Old South, was raised in Mississippi. He had that intriguing southern accent, at least to those not used to it. He'd worked on the Liberty-White Railroad, a 20-mile long narrow-gauge passenger and timber carrying line, established in 1902, but abandoned in 1921. It ran between Liberty and McComb, in the southwestern part of the state. In 1920, with the end of his job in sight, Red had learned of the Denver & Rio Grande Western as an excellent place to work, a job with a future. After he'd come west and gotten a job, they'd ordered the new K-36's, and it seemed he'd made a good move. He was happy, though he missed fried chicken and grits some.

Circus trains were sometimes transported on the railroad between towns, and Red had worked as a brakeman on several of those occasions. More than one elephant had been a passenger. That poor creature was the subject of some of Red's humor or attempt at such.

"Hey, Eli, why does an elephant not like to ride the train?" asked Red grinning.

"I don't know, Red, but I'm sure you're gonna tell me," replied Eli, a bit wearily.

"Because it doesn't like leaving its trunk in the baggage car!" answered Red, smiling.

Gee, Red, you'd think I'd know the answer since you've asked me a dozen times or more, thought Eli.

"Hey Sam, people are always asking why we have a schedule if we're never on time. Why do you think we have one?"

"Not sure, Red," Sam responded, thinking *he's gonna tell me why, for sure.*

"Well, if we didn't have a schedule, no one would ever know we were late!" smirked Red.

Woohoo, thought Sam.

"Hey fellows, the passengers always want to know how fast we're going. Here's what I tell them to explain that we don't go that fast. One day we stopped for a cow on the tracks. Finally, we got the cow out of the way. We went another 15 minutes and had to stop again. I asked the conductor why we stopped again, and he said, we caught up to that same cow!" Haha haha haha! Red laughed.

Isn't there something you need to be doing at the back of the train, wondered Eli?

"Hey, guys, when can a rabbit can go faster than the train?" asked Red.

Eli and Sam both pretended not to hear so as not to have to reply, but no matter. Red provided the answer.

"When he's on the train and running forward!" chuckled Red.

"What kind of bubble gum does the railroad make?" "Chew, chew!" "What is as big as the locomotive, goes the same speed, but is weightless?" "Its shadow!" "Why can't the locomotive sit down after a long trip like this?" "It has a tender behind!" "Why can't the whole train sit down after a long trip like this?" "It has a red caboose!" "What happened when the passenger took the 5:15 pm train home?" "He had to bring it back!" "How do you find a lost train?" "Follow its tracks!"

"I've meant to write all these down for you, but I keep getting sidetracked," added Red, with a har har har. *Can't wait for that*, Eli worn down by then, sighed.

After a lull in Griffin's running narrative, during which he attended to some brakeman duties, Red asked Eli and Sam in a serious way if they'd heard about the geologist who'd had trouble in Rock Tunnel recently. The man, according to brakeman Griffin, had brought his wife along to help gather rock samples.

The men in the cab took the bait. It was indeed news to them. "He took her for granite," Red explained with a poker face, "and she left him."

And on and on and on.

Red was a fine brakeman, though. And he was good to have along on tiring late-night trips; he kept you awake. Over a career, there were those few scary moments when someone was running ahead or behind schedule – it might be you – and a quick dash into a siding was suddenly necessary. Maybe when a headlight could be seen coming at you from far or even near.

A head brakeman who could exit a moving locomotive in a sure-footed way, dash to the switch across wet rails, insert his key, unlock the switch and reposition it, and have you in the siding before the train passed in the opposite direction, was invaluable, and Red was one of those. So his kidding around was tolerated.

Some things had happened that neither The Public

nor the Denver & Rio Grande Western bosses didn't know about, and wouldn't find out. But trainmen knew and knew who they could count on, and if having that person along meant listening to a few bad jokes over and over, so be it.

On the line, a man was allowed his personality, his quirky behavior, so long as he worked as a professional to help get the train to its destination safely and on schedule. So long as he was trustworthy.

Many things happened over a career on the tracks, some of them good, some of them not good. Sometimes men even told lies, covered things up. But when men did their best, even though there were mistakes, they left it all on the line knowing they'd acted with honor and good intention. The lies and errors were covered over with mutual respect. The bosses didn't have to know everything.

18

CHAMA TIME

They continued towards Chama. The hand brakes, those controlled by the wheel on the 'B' end of the cars, the Brake end, were set to drag a little. It was called retarding the brakes. They would smoke some, smell some, but that was normal. Just don't let them get too hot, please, brakemen.

The air furnished by a steam-powered compressor produces up to 90 pounds of air pressure. Between 70 and 90 are needed for the braking system. So watch the air pressure.

Eli proceeded downhill slowly, not exceeding 12 mph, usually closer to 8 mph. Around Windy Point he drove, giving passengers a very scenic view of Wolf Creek Valley. The smooth sides of the valley indicated glacial activity long ago.

The big rocks on the right were a part of the Conejos formation, more than 35 million years old. So he'd been told, who knew?

Around another corner to the left and he pulled the lever that allowed for a 'blowdown.' Steam blew out the side of the locomotive, something that always seemed to fascinate passengers. They often saw a rainbow when looking through the drops of steam into the sunlight. The mountain water used in the boiler was 'good and plenty' according to early experts but still contained minerals and other impurities. Mud, for example.

The blowdown, a routine running procedure to rid the boiler of those impurities, made it last longer. Boilers were costly to overhaul, and railroad maintenance officials were insistent that regular blowdowns be a part of the running procedure.

They ran downhill by Coxo. It wasn't a section headquarters; there were just a siding and a storage building. In the beginning, Coxo had been Codo, but once a telegraph operator couldn't read the "d," and in such cases, an "x" was substituted. Codo thus became Coxo for all time. Eli and Sam had wondered aloud, though not seriously, what if the "x" in Coxo couldn't be read? Would another "x" be substituted, and no one ever know? It was just a small bit of dry humor to pass the time and hadn't been funny the second time around.

Oh well.

The Cresco section house and encampment appeared beyond Coxo. They'd passed the section crew between the two "Cs," hard at work replacing some damaged ties. The Cresco tank was overflowing. It filled from a stream above the settlement. There was also a phone booth here, which, like the others, had an upgrade in recent years from just a telegraph key to having a telephone handset too. The equipment was for communication with Alamosa dispatch when necessary.

The Cresco water tank was mostly used when

necessary on a downhill run. The 4% grade in this area was apparent. It was easy to start the train from a full stop going downhill but not so easy when it was stretched out and headed uphill at this severe slant. Sometimes, though, the train had to make an uphill start.

Occasionally tent caterpillars invaded the aspen groves along this section of track, causing the train crew, if going uphill, to increase by two men. One sat on either side of the locomotive with a broom, sweeping off those insects so the engine could gain traction, friction and sand being inadequate to overcome the gooey mess under the driving wheels!

Now headed west, though, Hamilton's Point wasn't far away. There were springs throughout this area that kept the roadbed a bit damp and unstable; therefore, the speed limit was slower.

Caution was the order of the day, every day, at Hamilton's Point. Another place like Calico Cut.

They crossed Highway 17 for the third time on the 4% downgrade. There were no barriers that dropped and prevented a motor vehicle from crossing the tracks, just a simple X – Railroad Crossing sign. At the intersection, a Model T pickup was waiting, its bed loaded with something, maybe cattle feed. Eli and Sam couldn't tell what it was carrying.

The train rumbled on by Dalton's Crossing, the location of a lumber spur leading into the mountains. When the Denver & Rio Grande began operations in 1881 and opened up this country, the area – about 60 miles across each way with Chama at its rough center – had been covered with ponderosa pine. It was called the Chama Pinery.

The Dalton siding road led up to the headwaters of the Rio Chama, about five miles away. Ponderosa logs were still being hauled out, but the supply was rapidly dwindling as the area was being nearly clear-cut. Where would you now find the lumber cut from those timbers?

Just look in all the newly built houses in Denver, and most of it was there. Denver was growing rapidly. By 1927 its population was 275,000, and there was plenty of demand for new homes.

Not too far ahead and the train crossed the Lobato Trestle, of the same style of German design as the Cascade Trestle further back. Their fabrication took place in 1881 in Bethlehem, Pennsylvania. Both trestles had no cross-bracing and were restricted to one locomotive at a time, weight limitations to be safe.

It was 100 feet above the east fork of little Wolf Creek, and first-time passengers especially always oooohed and ahhhhhhed here, just as they did at Cascade.

On the right immediately ahead were cattle pens, used to corral sheep and cattle en route to market. Eli and Sam stopped there often with freights, loading those animals. The cows went into single-level cars. Sheep were short enough that two levels traveled together in one car. Any sheep with good sense knew it was best to be on the top floor if they didn't have a raincoat.

The next left turn took them into the Narrows. Above the Narrows, glaciers had come down both the Wolf Creek and Rio Chama valleys during the Ice Age but had blocked each other here in what was another terminal moraine. The glaciers remained and melted, so the Narrows was an area not glacially carved. But the roadbed was built on soft debris dropped from the ice when it dissolved, and as a result, deposited here. Thus the track took a lot of attention and maintenance.

Just before crossing Highway 17 one last time, above Chama, the 4% grade ended. Braking was not so critical after that, with a gentler slope as they'd roll into the yard.

Before getting into Chama, though, they'd cross the Rio Chama over the new bridge, erected in 1923, four years earlier. This beautiful steel structure, 230 feet long, replaced an original wood trestle.

As one approached the bridge, it wasn't unusual to look up into the massive ponderosa pine on the left and see a man with a camera. Mr. Fred Jukes, a renowned Western photographer, was often inclined to haul himself and his camera high into that tree to take aerial photos of the train.

If Mr. Jukes was up there, it was a good time to smile and wave!

19

FIRING UP AT FOSTER'S

Eli often spent time in Chama. The name translated to "here they have wrestled," but another interpretation was "here they have fought," leading some to believe it had been the site of warring Native Americans. Chama had grown from a small gathering of a few tents and houses along the Rio Chama in 1865 to a good-sized railroad town, as the headquarters of the 4th Division of the Denver & Rio Grande Western Railroad.

The town was first located along the river but flooded so often that residents finally moved the central portion higher onto a terrace, thus the name Terrace Avenue for the main street. The relocation solved the flooding problem. Fires were devastating to the new railroad town, occurring every few years. The worst was in 1899 when someone started a fire in Foster's rooming house. It spread southward then went to the east, pushed by a changing wind. Much of Chama was lost. The buildings were all wooden, were spaced closely together, and fire protection was next to nothing in that era.

Eli seldom drove west from Chama to Durango or on to Silverton. He was most valued as an engineer who could skillfully handle a train up the 12 mile 4% grade through Wolf Creek Valley to Cumbres Pass at 10,015 feet.

He and another engineer on a second locomotive could pull as many as 15 fully loaded freight cars up the big hill to the siding at Cumbres, where the cars were assembled into much longer trains for the trip to Antonito. From Cumbres Pass, the route descended at a more moderate rate of about 1%, so that the train lost about a foot for every 100 feet forward.

With that gradual descent, a long train, up to 50 cars, could then be tugged from Cumbres to Antonito by just one locomotive. One section of track between Los Pinos section house and Osier was almost level.

In Chama, Eli might stay in converted crew quarters made of an old boxcar, and most of the trainmen bunked there if they didn't have a home in the town. Eli usually saved money and slept in the boxcar, but he was single, earning good wages, and sometimes treated himself to a room at Foster's. The privacy was welcome. That establishment had been built in 1881 when the new railroad became fully operational and had been in business continuously since that time.

Foster's had both a café and a place to get a drink, and sometimes Eli would have a beer there, especially when Sam Gonzales was his fireman. It was another place where prohibition hadn't had much effect. They kept their drinking to a minimum, though, since both valued their jobs and their reputations, and anything out of line in town would quickly reach the ears of 4th Division superintendent Hawkins. His office was in the depot just down from Terrace Avenue. The depot that existed in 1927 was the one rebuilt after the devastating 1899 fire that destroyed the original.

Without a doubt, a man with money in his pockets to jingle in either Chama or Antonito or any railroad town for that matter could engage in almost any vice he chose. But if you had family close by, had grown up here or nearby, there were few secrets. If you valued your family name, you kept your shenanigans to a minimum. Such was the case with Eli and Sam. There were universal rules regarding all small towns that one was wise to consider:

If you didn't know what you were doing, surely there were many others who did.

In small towns, good people outnumber bad people from 100 to 1. In big towns, the 100 are nervous. But in small towns, it's the one.

A small town has as many eyes as does a fly.

There are no secrets in small towns, but there are no strangers, either.

It was said of small towns, people bought the local newspaper not to read the news, but to see if the editor had the story right.

Eli attended mass at St. Michael's Catholic Church in Chama when his schedule allowed. He liked the people and thought if he ever wanted to live someplace besides Conejos or Antonito, then Chama, New Mexico, would be his choice.

He'd even spotted a little Chama house he liked. It was for sale although rented at present. It was on Terrace Avenue just south of the business area. The home was sturdily constructed, mostly out of used rail ties.

After Arri came along or at the least, the thought of her sharing his life developed, Eli thought how great it would be to live out his days with her in that house. Many people thought that living next to the noisy trains would be a bother, but Eliseo Martinez believed that nothing would make for better listening than the music of the rails.

Even the sound of a night whistle up at the last crossing of Highway 17, just above Chama. It was such a lonesome and soulful sound in the dark.

But Eli didn't think he'd be lonesome if Arriana were by his side, in that little Chama house.

20

RIGHT WELL

On July 12th, engineer Martinez received a special train order, out of the ordinary. He was to report to Antonito on July 16th, to drive # 488 light to Denver. What tha...?

Eli knew that very heavy maintenance was done in the Denver shops. The '88 had recently been involved in a derailing and was thought to have frame damage that, if not repaired, would lead to extensive wear and tear. Only two years old, it was due to serve for many more decades.

The Baldwin Locomotive Works in Philadelphia, Pennsylvania, made all the K-27's, K-28's, and K-36's currently used by the Denver & Rio Grande Western. To facilitate repair of engines on-site, Baldwin stationed expert technical advisers at the railroad customer's major maintenance facilities. They were well trained in all phases of locomotive repair and would assist railroad mechanics in unusual situations. The frame repair for #488 was one of those.

Fireman Evan Adame was to accompany Eli on the trip. Adame was 38, a senior employee, dual qualified as both engineer and fireman.

Eli didn't think that Evan Adame needed his help to get this job done.

Eli discussed it with several folks and, of course, with Sam Gonzales, his regular fireman.

Sam knew the score, he thought.

"Why, Eli, you've been picked as a Chosen One! What they do is this...the engineers they have their eye on for the future for the route from Denver south and west through the line, the ones who pull folks like touring European royalty, are brought to Denver on sort of a test trip."

"Sure, Evan can do the job, they already know that. He's there to see if you can, to give you pointers along the way, to furnish a report to the big bosses when you get there, unofficially and officially, too, depending on how you look at it. Do well, and you are 'In like Flynn', my friend! Congratulations!" said Sam, excited and smiling.

Well before the given time, since Eli wanted to be not only on time but early for this run, he appeared at Antonito. The '88 was steamed up, just the tender attached. They'd be running light, no consist behind. The route to Denver could be done quickly since there was no weight to tug along.

They headed north, watering as necessary. Of course, Eli had been to Alamosa many times, so there was nothing new about getting there.

Eli already knew that his regular fireman, Sam Gonzales, was good at his job. It wasn't just a matter of throwing coal into the firebox. An expert fireman helped his engineer be a real professional. He anticipated the need for more or less steam, more or less fire. He didn't add coal to the extent the fire choked out but knew how to apply the controls in his charge when the fire needed it. He knew when to begin cooling the flame down to save coal when the destination was close.

He offered sound advice when it was opportune and never would embarrass the engineer in front of others, but would take him aside and give information discreetly. It was wise to listen to such a person. It was like being in the military service, Eli had heard, where a young military man should pay strict attention to the wise old enlisted sergeants who had been there, done that. In that way, one avoided making past mistakes while gaining respect.

In Evan Adame, Eli recognized a master before many miles were behind them. Eli learned that Evan had previously worked as an engineer on one of the most spectacular railroads in the West, the Alamogordo & Sacramento Mountain Railway between Alamogordo and Cloudcroft, New Mexico. That line, completed to Cloudcroft in 1900, gained over 4,000 feet elevation in 16 miles. There were grades up to 6.4% on which the company used Baldwin and Shay locomotives. They carried passengers and hauled timber. Evan applied and was accepted for employment with the Denver & Rio Grande Western when they ordered the ten new K-36's, a good indicator that a better future was possible. And his new employers treated him very well.

From Antonito to Denver was 280 miles. The distance markers were on the left side of the locomotive. They passed swiftly. Much of the grade was level, straight. It was easy to run up to 30 mph.

Much different from the 64 miles from Antonito to Chama in the San Juan Mountains, where the only straight sections were at the beginning of the trip for a couple of miles, at the end of the journey for about that same distance, and a mile and one half in the middle in the Los Pinos Valley.

They'd departed Antonito at daybreak, 6 am. They pushed through stations above Alamosa – Ft. Garland – La Veta – Walsenburg – Pueblo – finally to Colorado Springs just before dark. Their orders called for an overnight stop there, why run at night when you didn't need to? The '88 wasn't scheduled into the shop for a couple more days. Eli had noticed that the train orders were generous with the time allowed to reach Denver on this trip. The journey back wasn't scheduled yet as the repair time was uncertain.

They'd gotten to Colorado Springs in nine hours. Eli had felt a bit of vibration in the '88 he hadn't noticed before, the result of the derailing, he guessed.

Eli had heard the old joke. What would happen between there and Denver to save your train if it was rolling backward, going fast and downhill too, the brakes off, disaster imminent, out of control? What would cushion the impact, save the day?

The Colorado Springs, of course. Haha.

General William Clayton Palmer, Civil War hero, winner of the Medal of Honor for his actions as a leader of Federal cavalry in a battle in Alabama in 1863, and the person who'd chartered the Denver & Rio Grande in 1870 had established this town in 1872. It had been the first stop reached on his new line, the first railroad town he'd laid out.

Evan Adame took Eli Martinez to a Colorado Springs hotel, where rooms awaited them. A nice place. Eli was impressed. They cleaned up then ate a good meal in the hotel's restaurant.

After dinner, Evan suggested they go to the Rusty Wrench for a nightcap, just one. They had an early first light start for Denver the next morning. The Wrench was a pretty nice place compared to Losario's Bar – okay, dance hall – where Eli and Sam Gonzales usually drank, to the extent they did.

They had a cold beer. Eli noticed some nice looking women circulating in the Rusty Wrench, being very friendly to the customers, most of who seemed to be railroad workers out on the town.

He glanced at one female in kind of a serious way. Eli had never 'been' with a woman and, like nearly all young men, was curious. After all, at 28, he was not so young any longer. Some might say Eliseo was overdue for such an experience. Long ago, he'd had 'the talk' with his dad, though his father seemed embarrassed and had only done so at the insistence of Eli's mother.

Eli's Uncle Charlie, his father's brother, was more open about things when he and Eli went on a camping and fishing trip to the Rio de Los Pinos. Uncle Charlie brought it up after they swigged a little moonshine along the edge of the River of the Pines. Eli had been uncomfortable, but his uncle had just laughed and told him, you'll figure it all out, Eli!

At the Rusty Wrench, Evan took Eli by the shoulder gently. He told Martinez they needed to ignore the women for now; they'd have time for that in Denver while they waited on the repair of the '88. They couldn't get into any trouble by having one cold beer, but they shouldn't push their luck. Eli shook his head to clear the distraction, thinking *Evan's right, gotta stick with business, don't want to mess up now.*

They were on their way at daybreak. It was a short

three hour run into Denver. Eli was amazed by the size of the yards and repair facilities, compared to anything he'd seen previously. With Evan's advice about track selection and directions, they eased into the roundhouse smoothly, and shut the '88 down to just a standing fire, waiting for the engine to be moved by yard crew into the appropriate stall.

Someone was there to meet them. Mr. Danson was a senior maintenance supervisor. He gave Eli a quick once-over and then glanced at Evan questioningly. Evan gave Danson a thumbs-up.

Eli caught that and realized he'd just gotten an initial sign of approval for how he'd conducted himself and driven the locomotive to Denver. He was inwardly pleased, though he realized there was much for him to learn about the company, a task he eagerly awaited. Suddenly his thoughts turned to Arri, how happy she'd be, how pleased he'd be to have pleased her with his job knowledge and performance. *Take that, Leo,* he thought. *You're not the only one who can be a star worker for the railroad!*

Mr. Danson disappeared with Evan while leaving a young assistant, Joshua, to show Eli the maintenance facilities. Eli and his host walked around and looked – the young man expertly advised Eli on the shop's capabilities. Much later, he would learn he'd met Joshua Bell, the grandson of General Palmer's main partner in the Denver & Rio Grande's initial charter, Dr. William Bell. They'd pulled out all the stops to take a good look at Eliseo Martinez, it seemed.

At lunch, Joshua, Mr. Danson, Evan, and Eli met at a diner within walking distance of the shops for a good meal. Afterward, they escorted Eli to the company's administrative offices where a young woman, Sonia Alvarez, gave him the nickel tour. She was a secretary in the main office. Eli was tongue-tied, a little self-conscious to be escorted by a woman, all the while as she acted with complete confidence. He'd read about how women were beginning to work in such jobs, to be self-sufficient, to go out at night, to even be sexually independent, but he only dared think about such things. She had lipstick on! Eli had heard of girls called Flappers. Was she one of those? They spent two hours together in their walkabout, including a coffee break.

Eli noticed that nearly all the other office girls were wearing lipstick or other cosmetics. In his mother's generation, such products were thought to be worn only by those women engaged in prostitution. It was another indication of the change in the wind during the Roaring 20s!

Sonia was non-plussed by it all, just another day at the office. The same couldn't be said for Eli, who was watching, learning, and experiencing new things. *Wow!* he thought. He didn't know it, but the 'how you gonna keep 'em down on the farm, when they've seen Paree?' song could have been playing for him right then!

After the tour, Sonia returned her charge, whose own batteries had been charged during his visit though he remained quiet, back to her office where Evan was waiting.

Sonia looked at Eli with interest, perhaps wondering if he might like to go dancing with a pretty girl while in Denver – but Eli, being from the hinterlands and not being used to this kind of place, remained the complete gentleman and said nothing but "thank you" to her. You don't have a clue, Eli Martinez, she thought, then smiled at him and excused herself.

Sonia wasn't a student, but she'd read articles and knew that the latest trend at colleges was 'petting.' The age of the automobile had, in essence, given students bedrooms on wheels. That and the new freedom now exercised by women had led to extensive sexual activity without actually having sexual intercourse. Sonia had wondered how Eli might look with her lipstick smeared all over his face.

Evan grinned. "Well, Eli, you look like a guy who needs a little relaxation. No train driving tomorrow. I say we head over to the Rambling Way and have supper and a few drinks tonight. It's a dance hall, a good place. What say?" Eli could think of no good reason to say no. Arri crossed his mind briefly, and he wished she were here with him, but since that was impossible, why not open himself up to the possibilities of the big city? So they left for the Ramblin', as everyone seemed to call it.

Once again, in spite of Prohibition, alcoholic drinks were readily available. They had one, then two, while having supper. Eli started to get a little buzz, to relax. He also noticed the number of outgoing, attractive women who were seemingly available. One of them reminded him of Sonia Alvarez though it wasn't her.

"Eli, we need to talk," said Evan. Eli sensed this was another part of Evan's current assignment. Eli was from the sticks compared to Denver, Colorado, but he wasn't stupid.

"It's natural to want to be with women even if you haven't been yet," Evan casually remarked. They were both feeling comfortable. "But you have a bright future with the company, and there are some things you need to know. Have you heard of gonorrhea? It's a disease."

Eli, of course, had not.

"If you begin to travel outside your home area, but even sometimes in Alamosa or Chama or even Antonito, you are going to run into women who seem to be very friendly. Life is hard for those who don't marry, who don't have other jobs, and often in desperation, they want to keep you company, for money. They might want you to pay for their rent. Trainmen have been known to have two families if they travel over long distances, one at either end of the line."

"Women who are with many men may have diseases. Those diseases – gonorrhea is one of them – may inflame your private parts, make you very sick. The worst of the diseases is syphilis, which can blind you, make you crazy, kill you. Do you understand?"

They were finishing their third drink now, and Eli was getting high and thought he understood too well because he was starting to look at one of the young women circulating in the crowd in a very determined kind of way.

"Eli, the railroad cannot and will not ever put anything in writing about it. The Public at large would get mad and not understand. But diseases like gonorrhea and syphilis can cost the company very much in the way of well-trained and valuable employees, not to mention bad public relations. Your bosses understand that young men wanting to be with young women is a natural thing. They remember being young themselves, and some of them act like they are still young."

"Do you follow me?" Evan asked.

"Yes sir," said Eli, the engineer to the fireman, the

engineer beginning to realize who was driving this particular train.

"The train's officials know that such women follow the train's construction schedule. Tent cities are set up around End of Track, wherever it is, and the railroad cannot do much about the women around End of Track. But it's different for the men who are permanent and more valuable employees, the men who see that the railroad makes a profit. Some of the married men are pillars of their community, active in their churches, and so forth. We must maintain a good image. It's true of all big companies. You can see also it would be an awful thing for those diseases to get home to the men's wives. Do you understand?"

"Yes, I do." *Eli slurred a little, but still seemed to have most of his wits about him,* Evan thought.

"Well, here's something you should know, you have to know, and it's not written down anywhere. You may never hear it from anyone but me. It's part of my job to tell you, and I like you, so here it is."

"The railroad calls women who come on to you - I'm not talking about End of Track but in places like division points, headquarters – the bigger cities usually – Railroad Women. Notice the initials? RW? What was the name of the bar we went into in Colorado Springs?"

Eli thought hard, a bit difficult to do now but remembered it was the Rusty Wrench.

"Notice the initials? RW? Same as Railroad Women," remarked Evan, with a quick wink.

"What's the name of this place?"

"Oh, the Rambling Way."

"Well, the initials are RW, right?"

The light bulb came on. RW. Railroad Women. Hmmm.

"The truth is, Eli, the railroad pays doctors to check these women out, at least once a month. The RW girls carry a card signed by the doctor that they've had an examination and are healthy. It's a whole lot cheaper for the railroad than training an engineer or valuable fireman or superintendent or skilled shop worker. You understand?"

Eli thought he did, in a confused kind of way. He nodded yes.

"So, no one is saying you have to be with these women. If you're a family man or even a single man with a good reputation, you are encouraged to maintain that good name in your community, to stay true to your wife if you have one. But if you choose to fool around, keep your fooling around in places with the initials of RW, get it? And you can even ask to see a girl's medical card if you want to."

Eli did get it, he thought. They sat in silence. Eli was amazed. He knew he was a sound engineer, and thought he was a quality person. Heck fire, he'd been an altar boy at Our Lady of the Guadalupe, the oldest church in Colorado, when he was a youngster in Conejos. Father O'Flanigan, their Irish priest, had taught Eli much.

But there was so much Eli didn't know, a lot that Father O'Flanigan had skipped. It seemed that Eli's special trip to Denver was special indeed. He sat there buzzed, thinking maybe it was time to learn a little more.

Leo Garcia had been to gay Paree and had learned there.

And Leo had Arri.

Why not?

Evan may have signaled to one of the prettiest girls circulating in the Rambling Way. She was the one that Eli thought kind of looked like Sonia. She had lipstick on, and it seemed to be Sonia's color.

Signal or not, she came over, approached Eli.

"Hi," she said quietly, seductively.

"Want to have a drink with me?"

Eli kind of lost his air, gulped, semi- choked, but got a yes out.

Evan excused himself, saying he needed to meet a friend somewhere else to conduct some business.

He was going over to the Runaway Wagon. "See you tomorrow at the shops, Eli. We don't need to be there until 10 am. Take your time, my friend."

Eli did.

He and the girl, who said her name was Angel – and she did look like one – had a drink and talked.

"Want to keep me company upstairs? We can simply talk. It's so loud here," she remarked, smiling at Eli.

At that moment, Eli Martinez wanted to keep her company for a lifetime. And suddenly, it did seem deafening here. If he'd been asked, he could have re- membered the name of Arriana Garcia only with great difficulty.

Eli followed Angel up the stairway, with a great deal of awkwardness. He knew that everyone in the Rambling Way was watching. He was sure that someone was run- ning down to the telegraph office at that very moment to send a message to his parents.

They were not, of course. It was a scene so familiar that no one really noticed, and Evan was already at the Runaway Wagon, conducting some business of his own.

Eli trailed Angel into Room 3. From this day forward, Eli would keep a special memory of the number 'three.' She closed the door. "Eli, you seem a little nervous, but don't be. Is this the first time you've been in a room by yourself with a girl? It's okay. All we have to do is talk. But I do need to get $3 from you, it's the cost of the room, and I have to give it to the barkeep when I go downstairs, or I will get in trouble."

Eli dug out three dollars and handed it to her. He'd have given her three hundred or even three thousand if she'd asked for it, and he'd had the money. Confusion reigned in his brain.

Angel would have been his Model A; at the moment, Eli didn't care.

They'd carried their drinks up with them.

She set her glass down and went over and looked Eli in the face. "Want to put your drink down, Eli?" Eli couldn't tell if she said that or purred it.

Eli actually couldn't remember at that moment if he had a hand, much less a drink in it, but he thrust a hand forward, and she took a glass that was in it and set it on a small table.

She slowly approached Eli and put her arms around his waist. She leaned against him, looking directly into his eyes. She kissed him gently at first. She stood on her tiptoes and nibbled on his left ear. Angel seemed to make sure that her breasts came into full contact with Eli's chest. Except for Arriana – who? – in the coal shed that one time, during which he'd almost fainted, he'd never kissed a woman on the lips. He had only kissed Maria on the cheek a couple of times at dances when no one was looking. And certainly not in a closed room with a woman being the only other person present. No one was looking now, he thought. He responded with a vigor he hadn't previously known was in him.

Eli saw the lights of gay Paree.

Things rapidly changed for him. Angel didn't seem too shocked, too bothered by it.

The truth was, she would have been more concerned if she hadn't gotten that reaction.

"Eli, you seem to want to do something else besides talk. We can do that, but it means I'll stay longer, and they expect $5 from me when I go downstairs so that I would need another $2 from you. Is that okay?"

Eli again removed his wallet from his pants with great difficulty since he was having trouble just breathing or maintaining his sense of balance and handed her $2, or it may have been two thousand, he wasn't sure.

She put it in her purse, which she'd placed on the little table. She reached down and carefully, slowly, unhooked Eli's belt. "Why don't you take those clothes off, Eli?"

Eli couldn't think of anything he would rather do instead. He sure didn't want to talk about Colorado's state flower or tree or bird.

Somehow he removed all his clothes without passing out. He wished he had a fig leaf. Angel stepped out of her garments.

Even though Eli was slightly drunk by now, his mind flashed back to a story he'd heard of the time a boy of 10 had walked to church with a young neighbor girl, 8. They had on their Sunday best and got to a creek which was brim-full.

They'd have to cross the creek to get to their respective churches. The little girl was Catholic, the boy Methodist. The girl, in complete innocence, suggested they undress to cross the creek, so their clothes didn't get wet. They did, going to their respective churches after redressing, then repeating that on their way home so as not to ruin their best clothes.

Returning home, the boy's mother asked him what he'd learned earlier by going to church.

"Mom, I didn't know until today there was so much difference between a Catholic and a Methodist," the boy replied.

Eli felt like that. He'd grown up with two sisters and his mother, and one bathroom in a small house. He'd had the usual accidental sightings of the female body, common in such situations. But this...

He'd never had a pretty young woman named Angel get naked in front of him while he got naked in front of her. With a bed in front of them.

Angel took him by the hand, led him over to the sink. "We need to wash you first, Eli. They want you to be clean while we talk."

"But I took a bath last night at the hotel, I'm clean," said Eli.

"That's good, Eli, but we need to make sure you're really clean," said Angel, smiling.

Oh, my goodness. Eli had never experienced such a thing. Later in life, he'd realize that the washing had probably been calculated to make the $5 coupling finish as quickly as possible.

Eli lay down with Angel. She showed him what to do, assisted him. Eli did it in what couldn't have been more than ten seconds max, undoubtedly less.

Later, back at his hotel room, Eli contemplated all that had happened. He was genuinely amazed. A thing talked about, thought about for years, and it was a beautiful thing, but it had been such a short time kind of thing. A quick something when slower would have been better.

As life went along, of course, Eli, now a 28-year-old non-virgin, would realize that his marriage proposal to Angel immediately after it had happened, his profession of love for her, had been a bit premature too, if that was the way to put it. But Eli's life had changed that night, as it does for all young men and women on the culmination of their first such event. After Angel said no to his proposal of marriage, in a kind understanding way really, after she reminded Eli it would be better for him to love someone who only wanted $5 to buy groceries with, after Angel said she was sorry but had to get back downstairs, or they would be mad at her, Eli got it. In more ways than one.

The truth was, Angel, whose real name was Penny Tompkins, had been flattered. Eli seemed like an exceptional person. Sure, he was backcountry, but he had a good heart, was genuine, down to earth. Had it been earlier in her life, in a different time and place, she would have given his impromptu proposal serious consideration. She'd have made him forget anyone named Arriana, whom he'd mentioned when they did talk briefly. But by now, there'd been too many men, too many stories, too much conniving, and twisting and turning to get by. Too much independence. It was hard now to imagine the quiet life of a wife and mother, and she didn't think she could adjust. Too much water down the river and not a river named the Rio de Los Pinos either. So it wouldn't have worked, regardless.

There were other factors at play during the Roaring

'20s, which affected young women's thinking, things that Eli and Leo and other men for that matter didn't stop to consider. WWI was one of the deadliest conflicts in history. Between 9 and 11 million soldiers died in combat. There were about 30 million civilian deaths.

Then in 1918, immediately following the Great War, a world-wide Spanish flu epidemic occurred. As many as 500 million persons were affected, one in three of the planet's population. Some 20 to 50 million people died, including 675,000 Americans. Both these events, highly publicized, promoted in young people a feeling that life is short and could end at any moment. Young women thought about all that, and now some wanted to spend their youth enjoying their life and freedom. The undesirable alternative for many was staying home and waiting for traditional marriage. Whatever her lifestyle, Penny Tompkins – 'Angel' - was one of the former.

Goodbye, Eli, and good luck, and I appreciate you asking, she thought. *Have a good life, and thanks for being a gentleman while you were with me. You are an exception to the rule.*

The next morning, Eli met Evan at the appointed time, 10 am. Eli had a biscuit and coffee at a diner on the way. Evan looked at him curiously. Eli returned the look shyly, and Evan didn't need to ask him but knew that his introduction of Eli into the ways of manhood had happened, and he hoped it had gone well.

Evan thought back to his initiation into that rite of passage. It seemed so long ago but was a pleasant memory.

Eli and Evan stayed three more days. Eli abstained

the next night but was curious again the night after that. He went back to the Rambling Way, $5 conveniently tucked in his shirt pocket. Angel wasn't there, but Gloria was. She was pretty too. Eli knew a little more about what to expect. This time he got ten additional seconds for his money. And some advice.

"Eli," said Gloria," if you want things to last longer, you may have to think of something else besides what you're doing while you're doing it. Do you like ice cream? Do you like cake? Do you like eating a 2" thick steak?"

Of course, was Eli's reply.

"Then think of those things while you're doing it, distract yourself. Concentrate on them in your head, picture them, and say them over and over. Ice cream and cake and a 2" steak. Ice cream and cake and a 2" steak. Ice cream and cake and a 2" steak...like that," Gloria advised.

It was a good suggestion that Eli would always remember. And he managed to depart without proposing. "Thank you," he said to Gloria, leaving. Life was moving right along.

He and Evan returned the '88 to Antonito. While Eli briefly reflected on his time with Angel and Gloria, he quickly turned his thoughts to Arri. Finally, he could readily remember her name clearly. The real world hit him solidly in the face, dancing girls left behind. What a beautiful thing it would be to be with Arriana! He was motivated to get the show on the road. Had Leo Garcia been hitting her, mistreating her, again?

Suddenly his anger flared up once more as he thought of that. *That son of a bitch!*

Over the next few days, he was conscious of his

private parts as he performed normal functions, but all seemed to be okay, and soon, he guessed that all was well.

Right Well. RW, for sure.

21

THE HOT TUB CAPER

When Eli had been in the administrative offices of the Denver & Rio Grande Western in Denver, a Mr. Billings, who was in charge of recruiting and selection of section foremen, asked Eli something that made him think.

Billings recognized the importance of having good people, both supervising and feeding section crews, and wondered what Eli might have noticed that could help those folks.

It was a lonely, hard job, and once good people were in place, the company liked them to stay.

A section foreman's wife had her hands full with just keeping the crew fed but also had her wifely duties. One was washing her husband's clothes. Some of the section crew were willing to pay the woman to clean theirs as well, affording a source of extra money for her household or her savings. Some women liked to squirrel away a little cash for themselves. No one could predict the future. If anything happened to their husband, they were in trouble.

Once Eli had watched the Osier foreman's wife move her washtub out by the tracks where the locomotive stopped for watering. She'd given the engineer a sad little smile and asked him if he'd fill up her washtub with steaming hot water from the boiler.

She'd had a tub full of her husband's dirty clothes - working around coal dust and other dirt all day every day made for some dirty laundry. She had no machine to help her, merely a scrub board. Then after scrubbing, she had to wring out the clothes then hang them out to dry. And that was during summertime or weather warm enough for outdoor drying. Winter presented its added problems – a drying line had to be jury-rigged close to the coal heater inside.

Most of the time, there was boiler water to spare since the tender was being topped up, and the water replenished quickly and easily. Eli explained this to Mr. Billings and told him that such a practice if officially directed and when sufficient hot water was available, would be a helpful and popular thing with the wives who did laundry. It might seem like a small thing to a man in a Denver office, but out there in the world by the tracks...well, it would be a big help.

Eli had an ulterior motive. He'd wanted to start doing that on his own at Sublette to help Arriana – and to see her – but it would have been highly suspect if the section foreman hadn't received news of such a practice prearranged by the home office.

If Denver mandated such a thing, though, it was just another order to follow from the head shed.

Mr. Billings had liked the idea and said he'd issue such an order right away. It would be in the field within two weeks. It wouldn't require the trains to make a special stop and provide water, just at regular watering stops. And Sublette was a place where Eli stopped often.

Eli and other engineers knew the directive was in force when they saw washtubs out by the tracks.

Approaching Sublette while driving the westbound Express two weeks later, sure enough, there stood Arri beside her tub, heaped with dirty clothes.

Eli had made his customary signature greeting, so Arriana knew who was at the controls.

Sam smiled to himself. No dummy, he noticed this new washtub thing had soon begun after Eli, the new railroad Wonder Boy, had been to Denver. Coincidence? Maybe, maybe not. But odd.

Of course, the tub, filled with hot water and a big load of laundry, was heavy. It made perfect sense for Eli to hop down while Sam watered up, and with the help of a brakeman, move the whole contraption back to the clothesline at the rear of the house.

Leo Garcia was nowhere in sight.

Eli sent the brakeman on his way and remained with Arri for a couple of minutes. He looked her square in the eyes, seemingly with some new confidence he'd gained around women since she'd last seen him. That puzzled her a bit in a positive way, and she felt a surge of emotion along with a strange warm feeling which didn't seem just to come from the steaming tub of water fresh off the '87, Eli's fair steed today.

"It's good to see you, Arri. I've missed you." At that, Eli went kind of cold, but the way he looked at her said a whole lot more.

Arri blushed and smiled. "I've missed you too, Eli. I think of you. Be safe on your trip. For the first time, I'll look forward to doing the laundry. Thank you for your help."

"For you, Arri, anytime. Anything I can do for you – "ANYTHING," he said with emphasis – let me know. I will do it. Be safe yourself. So long."

Eli turned, resisted the impulse to jump into the air and click his heels, and walked back to the cab. He gave her another look as he pulled out, saw that she met his gaze directly. Eli didn't see any fresh bruises this time, but two from before still were visible, and Eli was unhappy once again about that.

Sam shoveled coal into the firebox. He glanced at Eli, nodded in the affirmative, winked, and smiled. Eli grinned back, sheepishly. Those looks between them signaled an understanding, and there was no longer any doubt in Sam's mind that Eliseo Martinez, railroad engineer first class, was smitten.

Sam looked down, though, and his smile faded as he wondered how this was going to play out.

It can't be good, he thought. *It can't be good at all.*

Short of Leo Garcia, section foreman – tough guy – a war hero – having a fatal heart attack out on the line, Sam could think of no easy solution.

22

UP IN SMOKE

Eli and Sam had exciting experiences while driving the train, some out of the ordinary. They were familiar with the Denver & Rio Grande's past; how it had changed the country where they lived. Their formal training had required them to learn the history, so they, their bosses said, could relate to The Public.

Eliseo Martinez was proud of his ability to drive the Colorado and New Mexico Express passenger trains and make The Public happy. At least he tried. If the truth is known, most of the trainmen preferred to drive freights. They might bounce or jostle cattle and sheep, even hogs, but a cow or sheep or pig was never in a hurry, never griped about the ride even if it was rough. They may have mooed, bleated, or grunted in disapproval, but they never complained to the bosses. That was a big reason that Eli and Sam did their best with the animals, truthfully. Besides, they knew the critters were headed for their last roundup and deserved a good final day.

People, by contrast, were always in a hurry, always

wanting the greatest comforts. Speed was all-important. But they also paid for tickets, bought building lots and houses in railroad towns, invested in the railroad itself, and it couldn't survive financially without them. So Eli and Sam did the best job they could and took pride in doing so.

The railroad was critical to their world in the San Juan Mountains, and north to Denver. Before the Denver & Rio Grande came, a trip from Denver to Durango, Colorado, took a few months on the seat of a wagon or the back of a horse or mule, longer on foot. The first settlers traveling west from Antonito, pursuing either good land or gold or silver or all three, had a rough time of it. There were no roads in the late 1870s on which to transport the valuable ore discovered north of Durango. Proceeding west from Cumbres Pass, those first folks had to lower their wagons down steep embankments by rope. It was a herculean effort.

Later some enterprising individuals, wanting to improve on Native American game trails, established toll roads. By 1874, there was such a road between the Chama Valley and San Luis Valley. The tollgate keeper, Mr. William Jenkins, set up shop at Osier, Colorado. He had a saloon, sold food, and kept a boarding house. He charged a small fee for anyone or anything – like animals – coming through the tollgate. The other choice was going up through the high mountains, not a reasonable or popular alternative. So most people paid the tolls, just a few cents. Like it or not, this was common practice in the Old West.

When the railroad opened for business to Chama in January 1881 – service to Silverton wasn't completed until 1882 – suddenly that months-long ride from

Denver could be completed in 24 hours, for a bit more than $20.00. The Denver & Rio Grande changed the nature of the country. Some called the D&RG the "little train" since it ran on 3-foot narrow gauge rails instead of 4 feet 8 ½ inch standard gauge. But there were good reasons it did. General Palmer and his backers could build the narrow gauge cheaper and quicker, and very importantly in the San Juans, the smaller track could more easily navigate turns in the mountains, on rails that were always curving.

From the start of operations in Antonito during 1880 up until 1927, as Eli and Sam drove their trains, nearly 50 years had passed during which the railroad had made money – and sometimes lost it – hauling mineral ore, passengers, cattle, sheep, hogs, fruit, produce, coal, lumber, motor cars, the US mail, and other freight. Profit in carrying silver ore virtually came to a halt in 1893 when the US government repealed the Silver Purchase Act. But the variety of revenue sources kept the line alive. Meanwhile, the people it served came to rely on it so that it became essential to their daily existence. How important a part is illustrated by one unusual set of train orders Eli and Sam received during June 1927.

Engineer Martinez and fireman Gonzales were to drive the New Mexico Express, the Westbound, to Chama on June 14th. The conductor, Mas Jay Martin, in overall charge of the train, met with all crew in Antonito. "Look at these orders, boys," said Mas, called No Mas by all who knew him well but sometimes just No which certainly confused any first-time passengers who could see that trainmen were doing what No said but saying No to him when he gave orders which yes, they'd follow. Oh well. It seemed to work.

"A passenger who'd ridden the train over his lifetime since it opened in 1881 died last December," explained No, "and the train was so important to him and his family, he wants his ashes put into the firebox. His name was Thomas Whitehead, his nickname was Choo Choo. The family has gotten permission from Denver. Our photographer Fred Jukes is on board to take some pictures. The Denver & Rio Grande will publicize the event. We're to bring the train to a standstill for a few minutes at the west portal of Rock Tunnel, by the Garfield monument, and be on our best behavior while it happens. Eli, stop the locomotive there just outside the tunnel – we don't want the smoke bunching up inside and choking the passengers."

"Our consist is six cars. Just get the last one out of the tunnel, so The Public isn't in the dark. Before we stop, I'll explain to them what will happen. Mr. Whitehead's daughter, Robyn, will toss his ashes in the box when you open it, Sam. Eli, give a long whistle salute to Mr. Whitehead. Thirty of his family members will be aboard. We'll stay there for about five minutes. After the whistle salute, we'll have a few moments of silence. When I say – Rest in peace, sir – that's your signal to sound your whistle for a start and move out to Osier. Professional now, men, the family is here. Any questions?" said No.

"No?" Sam, who sometimes couldn't resist, asked No Mas that way.

"What, Sam?" asked No.

"Are we going to stop again at the Jukes Tree and let Mr. Jukes climb up in it and take some more pictures?"

"Not today, Sam, Jukes will ride into Chama with us," No responded.

Yes, it was a good question for No as the crew often saw Mr. Jukes in the big ponderosa pine close to the new bridge over the Rio Chama, outside the Chama yard. If he was aboard, sometimes they stopped to let him off near the tree.

At the west portal, the ceremony was carried out in a dignified manner befitting Mr. Whitehead's last wishes. Cremations were not that common in 1927, and to a man, the train crew truly appreciated Mr. Whitehead honoring their train with his final request. It gave them pause for thought. None of the trainmen they knew had ever put their earthly remains in the firebox.

It was a thing they respected. For years afterward, men of the train crew who'd been aboard that day would sense the presence of Choo Choo Whitehead as they drove through the west portal overlooking mighty Toltec Gorge, where a small wisp of smoke always seemed to hang in the air.

Rest in peace, sir; they'd think when they saw it.

23

RUNAWAY WILLIE

Section foreman Leo Garcia knew that Jonas Barrio, the foreman at Toltec, just west of Sublette, was having problems. Mudslides had torn up the track there. Leo's gang was pretty well caught up or at least on schedule and doing routine preventive work. Leo thought it was time for him to get a pay raise and what better way to impress Mr. Hawkins, the superintendent, than to help Toltec get up to speed voluntarily.

He sent the boys west one day, three miles beyond their assigned area, to do some heavy work. There was some griping. And they'd already worked late finishing a job that shouldn't have been theirs. Willie Estrada was in the crew, and while he was a willing worker, he got caught up in the complaining with the rest of the men.

All of them were tired and hungry when they finally returned to Sublette. The strain was showing as they ate supper. Of course, it was hard on Arriana to feed them that late. The behind schedule cleanup even infringed on her preparation for the next morning's breakfast.

Leo picked up on the unhappiness of the crew. As they washed up to come inside the section house to eat, he overheard some of the serious bitching. Leo wasn't happy. He was the boss, and they would do what he told them to do, by damn!

After the meal, he went to both bunkhouses and told the men to gather in the bigger one. He read them the riot act. "I'm in charge!" he yelled. "I'm the boss, and you do what I tell you to do, or you can catch the next train to Antonito, and I'll hire someone to take your place!" he ranted. He'd overheard Willie griping too, unusual for him, and Leo singled him out for criticism.

"Willie, you're damned lucky to have this job. No one else will hire you. Cut out the belly-aching and get the work done or take a hike!" he bellowed, scaring the bejeebers out of him. Willie had the shell-shocked look of many of the young men Leo had seen in the trenches in France during the war.

Leo stalked out.

Willie took one of Leo's suggestions and took a hike. He ran away. Again.

Such criticism was just too much for him. He grabbed a few possessions and walked eastbound along the tracks. After about four miles, still walking in the darkness, he cut into the trees on the north side of the roadbed. He'd taken a few tins of airtights, mostly beans, and some peaches. He knew where there was a protective rock wall, the remnant of an old construction site from 1881. It had a fire pit and was sheltered from the wind, though it would be a pretty warm night because of the time of year.

Willie built a small fire, ate some canned food, drank some fresh water from a nearby stream, and lay down. He slept fitfully, thinking of how Leo had hollered at him. Estrada wondered about going back. Could he do it?

He debated returning for two more days and nights. Finally, on the third day, after he didn't come back, Leo Garcia realized he might have overdone it with Willie. The truth was, he had started to miss him being around after that short time because Willie was the one crew member who would do anything, and do it quickly when told.

Leo sent two men in opposite directions on speeders, beyond the limits of their section lines. They yelled Willie's name. The eastbound searchers spotted some boot prints in mud on the north side of the track about four miles out and yelled out. "Willie, we know you're there!"

"Mr. Garcia wants you back at work. He won't holler at you again. If you don't come on with us, he'll have to hire someone in your place. Your job is safe if you come back now."

Finally, Willie walked out, returned to Sublette with them. He was nervous as a cat at first, but Leo Garcia left him alone, didn't yell at him, and things soon were back to normal.

As normal as things got around the Sublette section gang crew, that is.

Behind his back, the other gang members nicknamed him Runaway Willie. The initials for that, of course, were RW. An odd twist.

Arri sensed that poor Willie was very anxious and was especially kind to him, asking him to help her and thanking him profusely to rebuild his confidence. Arriana Garcia's smile was just the tonic that Willie Estrada needed, and soon he was back to whatever Sublette usual was.

24

THE SCREAMER

On August 20, 1927, Eli was westbound with a freight, driving # 488. Sam Gonzales was ill with the flu, and Nacho Rivera was the fireman. Nacho was a long-time employee who'd started as a cleanup boy in the Chama shops. He was bright and a quick learner. He soon advanced through shop ranks to be a good maintenance man, but wanted to be riding on the train, not working on it.

Nacho applied to be a brakeman and, with his excellent employment record, was accepted and quickly learned that position too. But he still wasn't satisfied; he wanted to be in the cab. The conductor might be overall in charge, but Nacho wished to operate the controls!

He'd been working as a fireman for two years and was doing an excellent job. He was prompt to work and was honest, so much so that friends nicknamed him George – the saying was that if he chopped down a cherry tree, he'd have to confess his sin.

But they also said Nacho ate so much that his

confession wouldn't possibly take place until after he'd eaten all the cherries!

Regardless, Nacho was a very competent fireman who wanted more, to be an engineer. His prospects seemed bright, provided anything unusual didn't happen to sidetrack him, tired pun aside.

Eli and Nacho worked their way up the hill from Antonito, gaining that requisite 600 feet when they reached Lava Tank. It was a heavy freight, and the tender had been only ¾ full of water leaving Antonito. One train was already watering at Antonito, and another was waiting. So Alamosa dispatch had told them to get water at Lava.

OId Alvie Johnson would be glad they stopped, and would probably walk up and say hello after he was sure he'd gotten the water up from the Rio de Los Pinos. He had. He did.

He also had just received a vital telegram for Eli's freight, so important that if for any reason Eli had been bypassing the watering stop, Alvie was to flag the train to a halt.

The telegram explained there was a landslide at the west portal of Rock Tunnel, in the Osier district, and that the section foreman, Milton Southerall – everyone called him Milt – needed help and fast. At least two large boulders blocked the track. Eastbound traffic was stopped at Osier, west of the tunnel.

Dispatch directed Sublette foreman Leo Garcia to take two speeders and some men to help Milt. It was imperative to clear the tracks. Eli's train was to go to the east portal of Rock Tunnel and stop.

Engineer Martinez was to exit the cab, leaving the conductor in his usual control of the train, with Nacho tending the locomotive. Eli was to walk through the tunnel and check the work on the track to see if it was completely cleared and repaired as necessary for the train to pass safely. If Eli found Milt there, the engineer would question him as to whether the track was safe, ready for the train to proceed. If Milt and Leo were there, he should ask both of them, but Leo, between the two foremen, would have the final say. Such was Leo's status with the railroad.

If only Leo were there, as expected, he'd have the final say providing the engineer didn't receive unsatisfactory answers to his engine-related questions. Eliseo would be the final authority regarding the locomotive passing safely over the repaired area. The conductor, Isaiah Maximilian, in consultation with Eli, would make the final determination whether the train would proceed, considering all factors.

Telegram in hand, Eli and Nacho continued through Big Horn, reaching Sublette on schedule. Eli had sounded his new signature whistle. Nacho had ridden with engineer Martinez before and hadn't heard this sound, he thought, but oh well, things change. *Change seemed to be the only constant in life,* Nacho considered. Changes were always happening, and one had to deal with them or fall by the wayside.

The beautiful Mrs. Garcia was by the track with her washtub and load of dirty laundry. She also had a copy of the telegram that was sent to Eli's freight at Lava, in case he'd missed it there. Her instructions were to flag the freight down if it did not stop.

Eli had Nacho fill her tub with steaming water; then, Nacho helped Eli carry Mrs. Garcia's washtub to the back door. Nacho, like others, didn't at all mind gazing upon the beautiful Arriana Garcia for a few minutes. *Another perk of railroad employment* thought Nacho. *A real lady who limped who was so beautiful!*

Nacho noticed what was obvious, though. Mrs. Garcia had a big bruise on her left cheek. It looked fresh, and her right arm had new bruising on it too. He wondered if Eli had noticed those injuries. Hard not to. Nacho thought it an odd combination of physical damage for a single fall since the bruises were on opposite sides. He'd heard bunkhouse talk about the Garcias, stuff about the tough war hero and foreman who probably beat his wife, the pretty lady with one leg shorter than the other.

He glanced at Eli, who suddenly seemed about to have a blowdown, though he wasn't in the cab to operate the correct controls.

Ell was flushed, angry looking. Nacho saw Eli look at Mrs. Garcia with a questioning look, tilting his head sideways, raising his eyebrows, as if to ask: "Again?"

Worse yet, Nacho saw Arriana Garcia give a slight nod of the head – yes – then look down, breaking off eye contact with Eliseo.

When he was a brakeman, Nacho had voluntarily learned Morse Code to facilitate his advancement. The message couldn't have been more explicit if someone had tapped it out on a telegraph key.

There was something hidden, secret, and understood between Eli Martinez and Arriana Garcia.

Nacho was shocked. It wasn't unusual for a train crewman to have a friendly, nodding acquaintance with a section foreman's wife but this amount of intimate communication – well, goodness.

Eli and Nacho returned to the cab. The engineer

sounded two regular longs on the whistle, signifying a startup and engaged the throttle with a jolt, spinning the drive wheels. Not at all like Eli Martinez, star engineer, just recently returned from a special trip to Denver, Colorado.

The Denver & Rio Grande Western didn't like unnecessary wheel spinning, which could create a washboard on the track. Unneeded sliding on the wheels through hard braking was a no-no too since it could make a flat spot on the wheels.

Passing the western Sublette station limit, Eli gave a warning whistle burst – two longs and a short. The first long was Eli's now habitual AaaaaaaaaaaaahRiiiiiiiiiiiiiiiiiiiii!

Nacho thought it odd it sounded like Arri if you considered it carefully, no, probably just his imagination. But it hit him – Eli had recently changed his signature – he and Mrs. Garcia seemed to have some close understanding – it could be a secret communication between them!

Uh oh, thought Nacho. He hadn't suddenly been so nervous since a year ago when he'd nearly stepped on a giant Western Diamondback rattler while the train delayed at the Big Horn wye.

"I ought to kill him!" blurted out Eli as they drove westbound past the Toltec section house.

"Who, Eli?" asked Nacho, but he already thought he knew who Eli had in mind.

"Leo Garcia, that son of a bitch!"

Earlier at Sublette, while Nacho was standing near Eli and Mrs. Garcia, just after the head nod, he'd also overheard Eli ask her: "Where is he? Is he over there by Rock Tunnel?"

She'd told him yes, that Leo had been instructed in an earlier telegram to take two speeders and some men to help Milt Southerall clear the track of some fallen boulders as soon as possible. Leo had taken Willie Estrada and six more of the Sublette gang men and their tools on two speeders. They had left earlier that morning, should be working there by now.

They were.

Leo had taken Willie Estrada, Brett Jones, Justin Trujillo, Bryan Schofield, Adrian Macheco, Shorty Morales, and Rudy Vernon. When Leo and his gang got to the blocked track, Milt and his crew were already in place working. Leo's men helped the others clear the two large boulders from the roadbed. It wasn't easy, but by using what they called San Juan Toothpicks as pry bars, they finally sent the big rocks scuttling over the side into the depths of Toltec Gorge. The Toothpicks were worn-out Model T rear axles acquired for this kind of work.

Finishing that and with just smaller debris that littered the trestle and rails, Milt and his men left for Cascade Trestle – there was another pressing problem there.

Leo and his gang remained to finish up the work at Rock Tunnel.

There was no guardrail on the trestle. Leo assigned the men in teams of twos to work at clearing the smaller debris, directing them to observe each other for safety's sake. He kept Willie with him. Brett and Justin, who'd ridden the first speeder with Leo and Willie, were placed working next to the tunnel opening. Bryan and Adrian were put a few feet further along the track near the Garfield monument, with Shorty and

Rudy between the others. All were busy cleaning their respective areas, mostly with either their shovel tips or their hands to remove rock and dirt from between the ties. They were moving back and forth along the short section of track, bunched closely together.

Leo had nothing in his hands but stood daringly on the outer edge of the ties overlooking the gorge, facing the workers. Willie looked at him nervously. Willie didn't like being this close to the side, and Leo noticed his apprehension.

"Don't worry yourself, Willie," barked Leo, "I'm like a mountain goat. It doesn't bother me at all. Get over here closer to me. You need more practice working like this. The more you do it, the better you'll get at keeping your balance."

Willie cautiously moved over in Leo's direction but still wasn't comfortable being in such a dangerous place.

Bryan and Adrian, at that moment, were looking at the monument, thinking what a strange place for such a thing to be. Shorty and Rudy were laughing; Shorty had passed gas which lingered in the air, and Rudy was looking at Shorty, shaking his head with a "Man, did you have to do that?" look. Brett had just told Justin that they'd better keep an eye on Shorty to make sure he was working and not sleeping. There was a good reason they nicknamed him 'The Snorer,' and both were glancing in Shorty's direction, center track, at the entrance to the tunnel. All were occasionally moving back and forth, both east and west, doing their work.

It was a beehive of activity, though the bees were buzzing in a slow, deliberate way.

At the east portal of the tunnel, engineer Martinez,

as instructed, brought his freight to a stop, about 20 feet from the opening. The Osier section gang had posted a warning barricade in the event Eli's train had missed the telegrams. Eli left the engine with Nacho in charge, the train with Max.

He walked through the tunnel, between the tracks.

It was completely dry inside. Rock Tunnel was solid granite. The rock experts who traveled the train and studied such places said it was some of the oldest rock on earth, millions of years. He'd even heard the word 'billion' mentioned but had no idea how much that was — it had to be a very long time.

It was 366 feet through the tunnel. It was dark in the middle though Eli could see the opening at the west end. As he approached more of the daylight, his eyes, which had shut down in the darkness, began to open up.

Just to the left of the west portal, if one was westbound, was the 600-foot drop-off into Toltec Gorge, the highest point above the bottom of the canyon and the Rio de Los Pinos over which the train would pass.

The workers were milling around the area between the portal and the Garfield monument. There was an outcrop of rock, an overhang, and the men were actually between the outcropping and the portal. Eli's eyes adjusted to the light, and he recognized Leo Garcia and Willie Estrada, who were in the middle of the group, and two other men he knew from the Sublette gang, Bryan and Adrian – he didn't know their last names but thought those were their first names. Previously, he'd seen them around Sublette and out on the track.

Adrian was known to one and all as the 'Name Carver.' He'd worked out of several section gang locations and seemed to move from one to the other every two years or so. 'Adrian Macheco' was carved into hundreds of aspens along the right of way.

Eli had often thought maybe that's why he'd worked so many places. Each new supervisor would find out that he spent more time carving his name in trees than he did working, and probably encouraged him to move along to a different work gang.

All this was just remotely on Eli's mind, though. What was foremost in his thoughts were the fresh bruises on Arriana Garcia. He was not a happy camper.

Maybe, he thought, he could separate Leo from the others and say something about it. It was time to confront the issue, and there might never be a better opportunity.

It was no accident that Leo had taken Willie with him. The rest could have been any of the other Sublette crew. It didn't matter; they were all the same to Leo except for Willie.

Leo had gotten the telegraph message, which said the engineer on the westbound freight would be Eliseo Martinez. He'd heard snatches of the quiet talk; he'd noticed the difference in how Arriana looked at him when he'd bring up Eli's name. He thought there must be something going on between them.

Eli, that son of a bitch, had the nerve to talk to his wife! She was Leo's, no one else's!

The last straw for Leo had been overhearing two of the Sublette men joking about how Eliseo Martinez, Denver & Rio Grande Western star engineer, did more work carrying Mrs. Garcia's washtub than he did in the cab of the 480s! *That son of a bitch!*

Leo thought back to France, how he'd managed to

get the younger men, the new men, to go over the top of the trench first. He remembered how he'd used their bodies for shields, for cover from the German machine guns, how he'd survived. He'd survive this, by damn, and he'd get Eli Martinez to understand that Arriana was Leo's woman, and to hell with the engineer!

And he had Willie Estrada here with him to back up anything Leo said. Willie wouldn't dare do otherwise.

Eli approached Leo, who was still standing on the edge of the trestle, the 600-foot drop-off to his back. Leo had supreme confidence in his ability to deal with these heights. After all, he was the Sublette foreman, the most trusted and able foreman on the Denver & Rio Grande Western!

Eli stopped in front of Leo. He saw that the shovel men were clearing the last of some rocks and dirt from the roadway. There was sufficient clearance for the train to pass.

Willie was closest to Leo; the other men as a group were bunched together in the immediate area, busy with their hands and shovels, moving about.

"Looks like you're about ready for us," Eli guardedly told Leo.

"I'm ready for you, you bastard! You and me got to talk. Byan and Adrian, go down there by the monument, clear off the track there. The rest of you, get over by the tunnel. Get there now!" hollered Leo.

All the men heard the curse word, the tone of Leo's voice, and knew it was a good time to look another direction. That was their conditioned response to such behavior at Sublette when Leo got on the warpath. If you weren't the antelope the lion had singled out, it was good to make yourself scarce, muy pronto. All were close enough to be involved or to intervene, but did anyone want to?

All moved quickly, almost a blur, turning their backs to Leo, Eli, and Willie. They'd seen and heard all they wanted. This confrontation could get nasty. They were privy to the rumors.

Momentarily, there was one more sound, a scream that persisted for about four seconds. The men didn't know this, but a falling body traveling downwards through air fell about 200 feet per second after it accelerated to its maximum velocity.

It was 600 feet to the bottom of Toltec Gorge.

The scream echoed for several seconds more, but they'd heard a 'thunk' after about five seconds, time for a body to fall, hit, and for the sound to rebound back to them.

All of them jerked around immediately, saw Eli and Willie standing there, looking towards the edge.

Leo Garcia was nowhere in sight. If the gang had expected anyone to be missing, it would have been Eli, not Leo.

"Oh my God!" said Adrian, as realization set in.

"Holy Mary mother of Jesus!" breathed Bryan, feeling like he might pass out, barely able to speak. His knees shook, his legs trembled.

High on a ridgeline, on the north side of Toltec Gorge canyon, a bighorn sheep with extremely keen vision had seen it all, but would never say one word about it. All he knew about men was that they were always trying to kill him, so what if one went over the edge? No big deal.

25

TO THE MAX

No other person made a sound. Eli finally broke the silence and told Shorty Morales, who was closest to the tunnel entrance, to go and get Max, the conductor. There seemed to be no reason to try getting to the bottom of Toltec Gorge. Everyone knew that Leo Garcia was dead. No one could survive such a fall, not even Leo.

Rock Tunnel was three miles east of the section house at Osier. Max walked through the tunnel a little hesitantly when summoned and looked around at the west portal. It was strange to see the other men but not Leo. Max asked where Milt was. Someone quietly said Milt and his crew had left to work on the Cascade Trestle, west of Osier. Max told all of Leo's section men who were present to get on the two speeders and go to Osier and wait there for the train and further instructions.

He told them not to talk to the Osier crew about the incident but knew that wouldn't happen. It was hard to imagine anything else taking place that would be more of a topic of conversation.

Max returned to the train with Eli, who kind of stumbled along, once turning to Max almost through the tunnel and saying: "I didn't kill him, Max."

Max made no reply. At the locomotive, Max asked him if he was okay to drive the train into Osier and put it on the house track. Max knew that the three miles of rail between Rock Tunnel and Osier was level or nearly so and that if necessary, Nacho could drive the train in, especially with him and Eli reversing roles, with Eli there to help.

But Eli said: "It's my train, Max. I'll take her in. No one has to do my job."

They proceeded westbound to Osier.   Nacho watched Eli operate the controls. Eli seemed to be deep in thought and said nothing, except one time he looked at Nacho and said: "I didn't kill him, Nacho."

Nacho just nodded, didn't respond otherwise, and only remembered what Eli had said coming out of Sublette earlier that day: "I ought to kill that son of a bitch."

Nacho Rivera decided that Eli Martinez was a man of his word.

26

GO WEST, YOUNG MAN

At Osier, the train parked on the house track, the track closest to the depot, so the main line wasn't blocked. The train stopped midway, so there was room for other locomotives and cars at both ends. They were sure to have company.

Max and Milt Southerall, who'd come in with his crew from Cascade Trestle, talked over the situation. As foreman of the section of track where the incident happened, Max felt like Milt should take charge, but Milt didn't agree.

Mr. Hawkins, the 4th Division superintendent, had to be notified as soon as possible, and probably the Conejos County, Colorado, Sheriff's Department as well. In the past, there had been more than one survey of the border between Colorado and New Mexico, with the 37th parallel being the more or less official line, but presently the scene of Leo's death fell under the jurisdiction of Colorado.

"Max, Mr. Hawkins ordered your train to make contact with Leo and Milt, with Leo being the final decider over the track situation at Rock Tunnel. Hawkins gave your train orders as to how to proceed, to have engineer Martinez stop the train and walk through the tunnel to see if the repair was made. If the train hadn't been here, this couldn't have happened. You are in charge of the train, so you should notify Division."

Milt, adding a little sweetener to soothe the thing with Max, told him he had seniority on the Denver & Rio Grande by several years and that he knew that Max was best suited to take charge. Max reluctantly agreed and assumed responsibility.

He told all train crew and the seven men from the Sublette section gang that everyone would stay at Osier until Division headquarters sent further instructions. That was a given because unless someone left on a train or a speeder, there was nowhere to go. They should not discuss what happened among themselves, he said. He didn't mention that the Sheriff's Office would be summoned too, but the crewmen guessed that.

Isaiah Maximilian composed the following telegraph then sent it to the 4th Division at Chama. He sent a copy to the Conejos County Sheriff's Office. *The sooner the sheriff or a deputy arrived at Osier, the better,* thought Max.

The telegraph read:

8/20/27 1500 URGENT At 1415 hrs this dt, Sub Sec Frmn Leo Garcia, at Rock Tunnel on spcl trak assgnt, fell into Toltec Gorge from near west portal of Rock Tunnel, presumed dead. Circumstances req investigation. All present during incident standing by Osier. Req Conejos Co Sheriff Office send officers ASAP. Awaiting instruction. Signed – Isaiah Maximilian, Conductor, Train 872WBF, Eng 488

Max was a trained telegraph operator and sent the message himself. It immediately was delivered to Mr. Hawkins when received in Chama. Hawkins was at Foster's Café having a late lunch but so much for lunch. He quickly returned to the depot and had the following wire sent to Osier:

8/20/27 1515 URGENT I am en route. All remain in place. CCSO Sheriff Lee notified en route frm Anto spcl train. Immed have 8 Osier sect gng mbrs w/stretcher proceed Toltec Gorge to conf death and retrieve the body. Signed – George Hawkins 4th Div Supt Chama

Chama, Antonito, Alamosa, and Denver were frantic with activity, Denver headquarters having received copies of the telegrams too. This incident was an unusual happening, a potential disaster for the railroad in terms of public relations. The Public.

Along with the others, Willie Estrada had been ordered to stand by at Osier, but where could he go at any rate? The only way to leave would be on foot. And trains were coming from both directions, one from Chama with Mr. Hawkins aboard, the other from Antonito with Sheriff Lee or other deputies.

At Osier, Willie nervously paced, looked around in no particular direction. Mr. Hawkins, the big boss in Chama, was coming and would surely want to talk with Willie. All those important people headed this way, and they'd all want to talk to him. *It was bad enough to work for Mr. Garcia and have him yell at me,* Willie thought. *What will they say to me, what will they tell me to do?*

Willie thought about things. *Mr. Garcia was good to me in his way; he didn't give me as much trouble as he did the others. Mrs. Garcia was so helpful to me and always was kind to me. She'd let me help her with her housework, and she is so pretty, and she would smile at me. I know that Mr. Garcia shoved and pushed her around some and made bruises on her, but the same thing happened at my house when I was little, and no one cared.*

Willie fretted, dreaded the questions he knew were coming. He didn't think he could stand it. In the past, he'd run away to escape this kind of pressure, and it had worked.

Willie snuck away from the back of the section house, behind the bunkhouse, over behind the big coal platform. The old toll road was over that way. He ran down the hill and got on the road and started walking west. In a couple of miles, he walked past Cascade Trestle above him, jumped across tiny Cascade Creek, and kept going. Willie walked some more, keeping a careful eye on the tracks above. He figured they'd send someone out on a speeder both ways like they'd done before to find him.

This time, though, he wouldn't answer them. It wouldn't be Mr. Garcia he'd have to face, it would be Mr. Hawkins and the sheriff, people like that.

I can't go back, he thought.

He was up close to the tracks near the toll road, in use since 1874. He'd heard that a man named Jenkins had been the tollgate keeper at Osier; he'd heard that Jenkins had been a mean man. But Jenkins had been dead a long time, Willie believed. At least he knew he was no longer at Osier.

Willie crossed the tracks and headed uphill. He'd heard a noise, some people shouting, probably for him, he guessed a speeder was coming. Willie ran up the hill where some of the biggest of the bristlecone pines grew. He got behind one of the largest and crawled down low on the ground, underneath the branches on the uphill side.

It was getting darker, and the speeder went by. Willie knew they'd be back. In the Los Pinos Valley ahead, it would be hard to hide from anyone looking for him along the tracks. He climbed to the high ridge-line and followed it west, giving him a good view of the tracks both ways. In the past, he'd seen bighorn sheep up here, and he knew it was hard to get to them, so he felt safe.

Just before full dark, he saw the speeder returning eastbound. The men on it were mostly quiet, seemed they'd about given up finding him. Willie knew that the new Highway 17 was to the north, that it went over Manga Pass. He knew he'd have to find food in a day or two or would be too weak to walk much more.

There was plenty of good spring water to drink, so water was not a problem.

He thought his best chance of getting away was to get to the highway and stay away from the railroad. Willie slept that night in some brush and was a little cold but not so much.

Early the next morning, he found a stand of goose-berry bushes and ate berries for breakfast. He'd eaten them before when working out on the line and knew they were healthy.

He reached Highway 17 right at what he figured was noon. His stomach was surely telling him it was. Gooseberries weren't Mrs. Garcia's bacon and eggs.

He hid on a hilltop where the upcoming westbound traffic when there was any, would be going very slow while climbing. He had spent time in Antonito and thought he would recognize any motor vehicle belonging to the railroad that might be out looking for him, though he felt they might not believe he could have walked out to the highway and might not be looking there.

A Model T came along. It looked like a family, a full load of four people in the car. He decided not to show himself. The same thing happened again.

Then he saw a truck working its way up the steep grade. It had something in the back that looked like sacks of feed. There was just the driver. It was by now mid-afternoon, and Willie figured it was his best chance. He didn't want to get any hungrier than he already was. Estrada walked out to the road and stuck out his thumb. 'Hitching,' friends had called this. He was at the crest of the hill, or at least where it leveled out for a little way.

The driver, not anyone he knew, stopped and said: "Hop in! Glad for the company!" He started to ask Willie some questions. How did you get out here? Where are you going? But what little in the way of answers he got out of Willie soon told him that this young man, while seeming to be a harmless person, wasn't entirely playing with a full deck. So before long, he just left him alone, and they rode in silence.

Towards dark, not having reached Chama, the man stopped to eat supper, had some sandwiches he shared. Before they drove into town, Willie asked him to pull over and would have just jumped off if he had not. Willie skirted his way around Chama, over by Rabbit Peak. He knew there would be trainmen in the village who would recognize him, might know by now the railroad was looking for him. He worked his way around to the highway, got to Durango in a couple of days in the same manner, riding in another Model T truck with another driver hauling some lumber.

Willie Estrada didn't know where he was going, but he knew directions and thought that if he kept going west, away from where he'd come from back to the east, he'd get farther and farther away from those who were looking for him.

In this manner, Willie Estrada kept moving. Soon he was no stranger to hitchhiking on cars and trucks, and hopping a freight train had long been second nature. Along the rail lines, just out of the towns, Willie would find groups of fellow travelers, bumming their way across the country on their free mode of transportation. It was fun being King of the Road, he figured.

Willie did chores for food, shared supper, and lunch with other people headed the same direction. One time he felt uncomfortable as the train seemed headed not west but north, and he learned he had gotten to Utah. But another track headed in the direction of the sunset was found, and that one kept him pointed generally that way until the rails played out at San Diego, California. Other hikers told him he could go no farther, out there not too distant was the Pacific Ocean, water as far as you could see. Altogether, he'd been on the road for three weeks.

In San Diego, Willie found a job as a helper at a stable. John Sampson was a black man who'd done well for himself. John, who owned the stable and a blacksmith shop too, was slightly overwhelmed with work and could use an employee. When someone toiled for John, all they needed was a first name; he never bothered to ask for a last one. The friendly and willing-to-work Willie Estrada would do whatever task given and do it well. John wasn't used to that kind of attitude towards him as a black man and appreciated having Willie there.

Guillermo "Willie" Estrada began to settle into a comfortable routine in California and believed he could forget his former life, and he didn't have to answer any questions from the sheriff in Colorado or Mr. Hawkins, and he was happy about that.

27

GETTING THE
PRIORITIES STRAIGHT

Back in Osier the day Willie ran away, Sheriff Lee was coming from Conejos. The sheriff was bringing two deputies, Norbert Eldredge and David Sanchez, out of his six. There were a dozen or so people to question. A lot of investigating was required, an investigation that demanded professionalism. The foreman who was likely dead was a vital person for the Denver & Rio Grande Western. Plus, there was an election coming up in November. And all ducks had seemed to be in a row for Sheriff Juan Lee's reelection, the last term he planned to run.

Yes, it was time to retire after the next four years. All the men involved had family in the area; all were voters. This situation couldn't be messed up. It would probably be the most significant event of Sheriff Lee's time in office. He was a popular law enforcement official. Anglos in the area called him Johnny; Hispanics in light-hearted response called him Juanny. Of course, this was no light-hearted affair.

28

PICKING UP THE PIECES

The search team of eight Osier section gang hands assigned the job of finding and returning Leo Garcia's body left Osier just after first light the next morning after his apparent death. They rode speeders to within a mile of Rock Tunnel, then started a steep descent on foot to the bottom of Toltec Gorge.

The appointed leader, Moses Smithson, himself a World War I veteran though not decorated for combat like Leo, had been issued a Model A-1911 Browning .45 semi-automatic pistol fully loaded with nine rounds, in case of a need for a defensive weapon against something like a bear. Besides black bears, there were still some grizzlies around. It was the same type of personal sidearm he had used in WWI, so he was familiar with it.

Mr. Hawkins from Chama had told them to return Leo's body if possible.

Otherwise, they were to pick a burial site above the high water mark of the Rio de Los Pinos and give him as dignified a service as possible. One man brought a small Bible. Smithson, who had the pistol, also thought to bring along a small US flag, just in case.

No one knew for sure that Leo had died, of course, but it was almost certain he had. If he survived that fall and met them coming out while they were going in, General Palmer would probably give Garcia the railroad.

It took nearly all that day to reach the opening below where he'd fallen. There he lay, all right, certainly DRT, dead right there. His body was so torn up; it was difficult for even the war veteran to look. A few years had passed now since he'd seen such a horrible sight, and he'd just as soon have waited for a few more.

About 50 feet below the body lay a ball-peen hammer. That was a bit of a mystery to the men, but maybe someone had dropped it previously, although it was odd it wasn't rusty. Also scattered about in the gorge were various train parts from across the years – wheel and axle assemblies, pieces of bent railings, others. Not surprising.

Team members were determined to bring back what remained of Leo. They struggled courageously, but finally gave up and selected a small fairly level meadow a mile closer to Osier. It seemed a respectful place and was suitably above the water line.

The truth was, Leo had begun to smell. His smashed remains were seriously decomposing. It was no fun trying to haul him out.

All agreed that Leo had come far enough. They dug a grave with hand tools they had brought along. One of the men read a Bible passage as the others stood reverently with their hats off. The small US flag was placed on top of a canvas wrap that contained the body. A wooden cross made of driftwood marked the spot.

It was a nice gesture even though the next big flood would probably wash it away, leaving all traces of the gravesite lost.

The WWI vet wanted to fire a 21-gun salute. But they had just the one pistol and only nine rounds. The men agreed they might yet need some of the ammunition on the return trip and jointly decided that three shots would be fired, leaving six, a reasonable amount.

Bang! Bang! Bang!

The echoes of the shots were heard back in Osier, two miles away. One there could only guess why the team was shooting, but the explanation on their return made sense to those in charge. The right call, they said, very appropriate and something we can report to headquarters as a proper gesture to our war hero, Leo Garcia.

Moses Smithson, the man who led the search team for Leo's body, was later made the new section foreman at Sublette for his excellent work on the recovery team and the memorial service for Leo in the gorge. An announcement of all this went to The Public; after all, it was good public relations.

29

ON THE HOT SEAT

Mr. Hawkins arrived at Osier at 6 pm. He'd known the number of people remaining at Osier from Eli Martinez's train crew and the sheriff and whoever he brought along – indeed he'd summoned the coroner to accompany them – would tax the available food supply at the section house, so he had a Chama commissary officer put some additional supplies aboard a boxcar. Hawkins was in a coach that had some sleeping facilities, and his train consisted of that coach, the boxcar, engine # 464, and its tender – the '64 was a K-27, smaller than the 480 series K-36's.

Mr. Hawkins wired Alamosa Dispatch some basic instructions that told them to provide an engine for the sheriff and whoever the sheriff brought with him. Locomotive # 463 was at Antonito, and it came with a coach carrying the law enforcement people. At this time, Alamosa and all others were in the dark about what had happened at Osier but could imagine it was something terrible. The news spread like wildfire, and speculation was rampant. Best guess it involved engineer Eli Martinez's train since Alamosa knew it was stopped at Osier and would not be proceeding westbound anytime soon.

Many remembered recent rumors that had circulated regarding engineer Martinez and foreman Leo Garcia's wife.

The investigators were at Osier by 8 pm. They planned first to question Leo's Sublette section crew members who'd been present when Leo died. *Let's save the engineer for last,* Sheriff Lee thought. Maybe by then, they'd have a good idea of who'd pushed Leo Garcia to his death. If anyone had, that was. It could have been a slip, an accident, even a gust of wind, since Leo had been perched dangerously on the outer portion of the trestle, foolishly, so it seemed to nearly all present by now.

The men were separated and interviewed one by one.

Brett Jones said he and Justin Trujillo were in the center of the tracks, within almost touching distance of where Leo stood. Eli Martinez and Willie Estrada were closest. All of us were Gandy Dancing, explained Brett. The sheriff's men knew that Gandy was the name of the company that made shovels and that the construction men who used shovels were called Gandy Dancers.

"As you were using your shovel to pick up dirt and rocks and throw them over the side, could you have struck Leo and caused him to lose his balance? Your shovel handle is four feet long, five feet with the shovel itself," Norbie Eldridge asked this question, adding that last observation.

"Naw, I would have liked to but would have been afraid that the foreman would have grabbed my shovel and took me with him. That mean bastard fired my second cousin, Gerald Thule, last year and him and his wife have damn near starved to death. He can't find a job anywhere," said Brett. "Leo would have fired me too if he'd known me and Jerry was kin."

Justin said he didn't push Leo but didn't mind that it happened. "He was a tough one, always wanting to be the big man, and beat his wife too. She's a pretty lady who has always been nice to us, but we couldn't do anything to help her, or we'd either get hurt by Leo or sent packing. It ain't been a good place to work."

Both Brett and Justin admitted that the whole crew was moving around while they worked, and they couldn't remember the exact place that the others were when Leo went down, screaming. Justin and Brett agreed both had looked away when Leo cussed Eli Martinez. "Sometimes it was a good thing not to see too much, and it seemed like it was going to be one of those times, for sure," added Brett.

Justin said he had seen Leo mistreat many people, including Leo abusing Mrs. Garcia, and he always got away with it because he was a war hero, he figured. He long guessed something terrible would happen to Leo someday, and he wasn't sad about it, but that scream and thunk would be something he'd never forget.

Sheriff Lee thought, *Oh boy, this could be tougher than I believed at first. Leo Garcia must have been a real sumbitch away from where outside people could see him.*

Bryan Schofield, who was over closer to the monument with Adrian Macheco, the 'Name Carver', said that he and Adrian looked away too when they heard the cussing between Leo Garcia and Eli Martinez. He told the questioner that Adrian could always look away from whatever was going on because he was always looking for some new place to put his name. Schofield thought they'd been out of shovel reaching range but admitted they'd moved back and forth across the trestle to within a little distance of Leo and Willie and then Eli when a stray rock they'd tossed had not fallen down the gorge but had landed on the track. He said he didn't have anything to do with Garcia's death but wasn't going to cry about it. "A hard man to work for," said Bryan. "You never wished no good for him."

Adrian Macheco said he heard the cussing and looked away for a suitable place to put his name the next time he had some free time coming. He said he was tired of having Leo Garcia holler at him and that Garcia lately had them doing work out of their district, he guessed to get on the right side of the foreman's boss, so maybe Leo would get a raise. He said that about six months ago, Leo Garcia had told him to quit wasting time putting his name everywhere, nobody cared and it was stupid. Macheco admitted that since then, he'd dreamed about carving Leo Garcia's name onto a wood plank that would serve as a tombstone, so maybe this was his chance now, but no, he didn't kill the son of a bitch.

Rudy Vernon, who said he and Shorty Morales had been told to clean up the track close to the tunnel opening, said he could think of better people to kill than Leo Garcia. He wouldn't have minded but didn't have nothing to do with it. Vernon said he and Shorty had been laughing so Leo Garcia couldn't see them, about Shorty passing gas. "Shorty called his last fart a 'Leo,'" Rudy said, and it was all he could do to keep from laughing out loud. "I didn't like the man at all," added Vernon, "but he did give me a job, and that was something good about him. My folks in Conejos put out a lot of water for wildflowers at their house, and they give a lot to folks for funerals. Mrs. Garcia was nice to us, and for her sake, not Leo's, I'll see that there are some flowers for his funeral if he can be brought up here from the bottom and be buried."

Shorty said, "Hell no, I didn't kill him, and I'm pretty sure Rudy was too far away to push him. We had been moving around, but when we heard the cussing, Rudy and me looked back in the tunnel, sometimes it was good to look at something you couldn't see so that you couldn't see something you could see."

Sheriff Lee, Eldridge, and Sanchez all considered that. They asked all the men if they'd seen anyone push Garcia, and everyone said no. Four of them thought that the scream they'd heard had come from the engineer since they thought it was him that might go flying when the trouble started. They were surprised to see Eli Martinez still standing there as the scream, and then the thunk was heard. They said it took a couple or three seconds to realize that it was Leo missing from the trestle. Shorty said it sounded like a girl screaming, and he smiled a Mona Lisa smile about that.

Did any of them feel a sudden gust of wind? "Well," Rudy said, "Shorty's fart could have done it. It was a pretty strong gust. Or the smell could have quickly drifted over to Mr. Garcia and caused him to lose his balance, maybe he passed out for a second or two."

"It nearly caused me to fall off the trestle," added Rudy. Norbie Eldridge gave Rudy a hard look and told him he hoped that if it was proved he killed Garcia, and he had a noose around his neck, he'd wonder if Rudy would still be having fun, happy thoughts, making jokes. Rudy said, "Well, come to think of it, the noise I heard could have been Shorty snoring a quick snore, he might have been leaning on his shovel the way he usually does and fell asleep pretty fast, and that would prove he didn't push Leo over with his shovel since it was busy holding Shorty up, 'cause if Shorty had swung the shovel at him, Shorty would have fell over too since he wouldn't have had anything supporting him."

"You boys wait in the bunkhouse. We'll call you if we need you again," said Norbie.

What a bunch of idiots, Norbie thought.

They sent for Willie to question him. Sheriff Lee thought it almost unnecessary since he knew Willie Estrada always did Leo Garcia's bidding without complaint or question, and he knew that Willie was a simpleton. *A good man, but he didn't have much sense,* thought the sheriff.

Sheriff Lee and his deputies knew that for someone to have committed a crime, there must be two things: motivation and opportunity. The person had to have a reason to do it and the chance to do it. While opportunity would have been present for Willie as for Eli and the others, there would have been no reason for Willie to kill Leo. Estrada had a job that no one else would give him. He was treated like a pet by both Leo Garcia and Mrs. Garcia. Everyone knew that.

Some of the other men had admitted some motivation, although they didn't seem to realize it or to take it seriously.

But Willie was nowhere to be found.

"Runaway Willie strikes again," Shorty told the

sheriff and deputies. The men explained how Willie would take off at the slightest hint of anything hard to deal with, had done it before several times, and how he'd been nervously pacing and looking around as if for a place to run. The only eastbound or westbound trains that had gotten to Osier since Leo had died were still there, Shorty reminded everyone, so Willie had to be on foot. All the speeders were accounted for, too.

They figured he had run down into the canyon by the river or where the toll road was. He'd likely gone westbound and was hiding along the tracks since eastbound would take him through the Rock Tunnel down past Toltec Gorge. There were some bristlecone pines to the west along the route, about a hundred, and he was probably somewhere out there.

Sheriff Lee sarcastically wondered how they'd get along without Shorty Evans and the others to figure this out.

Mr. Hawkins sent men out on speeders both directions, but they couldn't get Willie to come out of hiding if he was out there. *The poor young man, loony it seems, is probably scared to death,* thought Hawkins.

Nacho Rivera, the fireman on Eli's trip this time, was the next person brought in for questioning. He would prove to be the star witness of the day.

Nacho was dreading the moment. The sheriff's deputies didn't think Nacho would have much worthwhile to say. They'd already learned he'd stayed back in the cab tending the locomotive when Eli left, per orders, to walk through Rock Tunnel to contact Leo and his crew.

Nacho Rivera was sweating like a bullet. "Relax, Rivera," Norbie Eldridge told him, with a little smile. But why was he so nervous?

Answering the deputy's questions honestly was the pivotal moment for Nacho. He and Eli weren't especially close friends, and this was everything - job, income, future, family to support. He had to say every word he'd heard from Eli. And his friends already jokingly sometimes called Nacho 'George' because he couldn't tell a lie. Poor Eli.

Nacho knew that Leo Garcia was a bully, and he hadn't liked him either, but would he have killed him? Well, he'd seen the injuries to Mrs. Garcia just earlier this day at Sublette and if he'd been in love with her, maybe.

Nacho was questioned about his and Eli's time together since they'd left Antonito earlier today.

He told of their water stop at Lava Tank, and of having received the telegram regarding the track blockage at Toltec Tunnel and the actions they were to take. He covered their stop at Sublette, telling Norbie that Mrs. Garcia had been out by the track with a copy of the same urgent telegram for their train. Also, he recalled helping her with her laundry tub. Hearing about the tub, Norbie's ears perked up, actually moved forward a fraction of an inch, to make sure he understood. It sounded a little personal.

"Tell me everything that happened at Sublette when stopped," said Norbie. It was the first he'd heard of the new directive from Denver telling engineers to help foremen's wives with hot water for their washtubs.

Nacho did and told of his suspicions about there being something between Mrs. Garcia and engineer Martinez.

That little devil named Motivation suddenly presented itself on one shoulder of Deputy Norbie Eldridge, and balancing it on his other shoulder was its evil twin, Opportunity.

Nacho told of the injuries that looked fresh on Mrs. Garcia. He recalled the engineer's reaction, his anger. He spoke of seeing Eli ask: "Where is he?" And he told of Mrs. Garcia answering that question.

He related Eli's continuing build-up of anger as they traveled westward, and of Eli's outburst as they went through the Toltec section.

"I ought to kill him!" said Eli, per Nacho's correct recollection.

Bingo! thought Norbie, who was yet to question Eli, but now looked forward to it, so far as solving a crime went. Figuring out what happened was what he did.

He dismissed Nacho and told Sheriff Lee and David Sanchez what he'd heard.

They brought Eli Martinez in.

Might as well hit the nail on the head, thought Norbie, out loud. The sheriff and David agreed. Why drag it out?

"Mr. Martinez, Nacho Rivera told us some things he heard you say earlier today. He said you told him about Leo Garcia, 'I ought to kill him.' Did you kill him?" asked Norbie.

Eli was stunned. "No!" he blurted out. But that lightning bolt question had set him back; the cat was out of the bag.

Norbie calmly came back. "Eli, I know you and your family. You are good people, but sometimes good people do bad things, for what they think are good reasons. I know you are a regular member of Our Lady of Guadalupe Catholic Church. You have been taught that if you speak the truth, the truth shall set you free. I even know that you were an altar boy there and that Father O'Flanigan is a family friend as well as your priest. Tell me truthfully about what happened and what led up to it."

Eli spilled his guts.

He described his involvement with Mrs. Garcia. He said that, yes, he did love her. He said he'd broken off his engagement with Maria Lopez over it. He said yes, he knew it was wrong to love a married woman, but that Leo Garcia was also wrong to have cruelly treated her like Leo had, and someone had to do something about it, and that was Eli's plan. But his thinking, he said, never involved deciding to kill Leo, and he hadn't done so, even though yes, he said earlier today that he ought to.

Eli remembered to himself that he'd previously told a couple of other people that he ought to kill Leo, but it didn't seem so important to spell that out to Norbie just then. It would be like pouring fuel on a fire that was already burning.

Eli concluded: "At the west portal of the tunnel, I was close to Leo, but there were several other men there too. Everyone was bunched around. Leo cursed me, and I turned away from him when he did. Things were happening so fast. I guess I was trying to decide what to do when I heard a scream. It lasted for a few seconds. I heard a sound that sounded like him hitting the bottom of the gorge. We all stood there, looking at each other. Shorty Morales was standing next to the tunnel opening, closest to the train. I told him to run back to the locomotive to tell Max, the conductor, who was in charge, what happened. You know what's gone on since then."

"Did you see anyone else push him?"

"No."

"Did you see anyone throw a shovel full of rocks and dirt towards him that might have hit him, or maybe see a shovelhead strike him and cause him to fall?"

"No."

"Did you see him lose his balance and fall?"

"No."

"Did you feel a strong wind that might have caused him to lose his balance?"

Detective Eldridge already knew from the other men's answers that this had not happened, but wanted to see if Eli suddenly remembered such a strong wind.

"No."

Norbie considered his situation. Eli admitted he'd said earlier today he ought to kill Leo Garcia. But he denied he had.

Eli Martinez had suddenly become the number one suspect. The little devil and his evil cohort sitting on Norbie's shoulders sat down, a smug look on their faces. They'd done their jobs and were ready to move on.

Sheriff Lee and his deputies held a powwow and connected all the pieces they had. They wanted to talk to Willie and find out what he'd seen. They didn't believe his witness testimony was critical, however, given his mental state, which was about a half bubble off level, but it was a base that should be covered.

Eliseo Martinez, a star engineer for the Denver & Rio Grande Western, was arrested on suspicion of murder.

He was kept in a locked and guarded room at the Osier section house that night, taken by train the next day to the Conejos County jail at Conejos, Colorado.

Much more investigation would take place over the next two or three weeks.

The deputies examined Eli's July 16th trip to Denver in detail. Evan Adame, the fireman who'd accompanied Eli, was questioned, and Eli's Railroad Women adventures came to light. Adame did not mention that Denver & Rio Grande Western executives were complicit in asking him to introduce engineer Martinez to the ways of the RW world. That would be kept confidential, though it was likely that sheriff's deputies were already aware of the practice.

They uncovered Eli's involvement in the new policy regarding the furnishing of hot boiler water for washtubs. Hmmm.

Among those interviewed later, of course, were Eli's regular train crew members, and naturally, Sam Gonzales, who fired for Eli more than anyone else, plus friends like Jose Villela.

Sam's reaction to being brought in for questioning was much like Nacho's had been. Sweaty, nervous.

Unlike Nacho, though, Sam was Eli's good friend. Or Gonzales certainly had been.

But Sam was a truthful man, and spilled the beans, as had Nacho. "Yes, he did tell me that he ought to kill Leo," said Sam. He added that Eli said that would happen if Leo Garcia hit her and hurt her again. Gonzales didn't have to mention that Leo had done so and that Nacho Rivera and Eli had seen evidence of it just before Leo's death. Sam hated himself for telling, but he had to have his job. And it looked like Eli had followed through with his threat, no matter how righteous the cause. Sam told everything he knew about Eli's relationship with Arriana Garcia and admitted that on several occasions, Eli said he loved her.

So far as he knew, though, Eli and Mrs. Garcia hadn't done anything but talk. Well, maybe kiss a little. Likewise, Jose Villela, Eliseo's good friend from Antonito, coughed up what Eli had said he ought to do to Leo Garcia. Oh boy, poor Eli.

All the information uncovered made the case clearer to the Conejos County Sheriff's Department. Sheriff Lee hated this stuff, the makings of which could undo or certainly erode support for him during an upcoming election, but it was part of the job.

The community didn't want murders taking place in its midst either, and a single man professing his love for a married woman – whose husband died after threats were made to kill him under certain conditions and those conditions had been satisfied - well, not right. So the case was tightened up, closed.

A BOLO – Be On the Look Out – for Willie Estrada in the Four Corners region – Colorado, Arizona, Utah, and New Mexico - hadn't turned him up. No one had come forward saying they'd seen him.

Arriana was interviewed and was close-mouthed, but confirmed that Leo had indeed abused her on the night before she saw Eli Martinez at Sublette on August 20th, just before Leo took wings. Her admission of having been beaten added another small nail to Eli's legal coffin, as it was since Eli had told three people he'd kill Leo if he mistreated Arriana again, and on August 20th Eli had just learned from Arriana that Leo had.

In another two weeks, the circuit court judge was in Alamosa, and Eli's trial took place.

The court heard the evidence. All 12 of the jury had

to vote to convict Eli, to believe he was guilty beyond a reasonable doubt. The first vote was 9 to 3 in favor of conviction. The jury met and deliberated two more days. Following that, two more jurors came around. It was then 11 to 1. In the next session, the lone dissenter caved in.

Eliseo Martinez was sentenced to die for Leo's murder, to hang by the neck until dead.

The judge scheduled his execution for October 14, 1927.

Father O'Flanigan visited Eli every day.

30

LAST DAY AT SUBLETTE

On the day of Leo's death, Arriana had seen Eli leave from Sublette with the westbound train after asking her: "Where is he?"

That day, she had worried about what might happen but could do nothing about it. When Leo arrived home, assuming he did, and she didn't have supper made for him and the men, there would be hell to pay. And she didn't need any more bruises.

She even had to chop some firewood for kindling. Coal made a good fire but was hard to start, and she needed small, easy-to-light pieces of wood she called splinters to get the flames going. She used an ax as heavy as a sledgehammer for this work, the only one she had. But it kept her strong, and one day, she thought, this strength may come in handy.

The day passed. No Leo, no section gang members who'd gone with him returned. Things weren't all bad. She only had to fix supper for five men. Their telegraph key was silent. After dark, an unscheduled westbound locomotive, K-28 # 478, arrived and parked on the

Sublette siding. There was just one coach. Mr. Yang, the man in charge of Antonito, came to her door.

Mr. Yang had brought Father O'Flanigan along. Together they told her of Leo's death. It was a surprise, but it bothered Arriana a little that the news didn't bother her a lot. She had married Leo with an expectation that she'd have a good married life with a man who loved her, but if he had, he'd had a strange way of showing it.

Now, she was never more relieved that she and Leo had had no children. She'd done everything she could to prevent that, and considered herself just plain lucky too she'd never gotten pregnant. Things would be a lot more complicated if that happened. Thank you, Lord, she quietly prayed.

They had brought along a man from Antonito who would act temporarily as the Sublette foreman and another man who would cook for the time being. Both would move into the section house until another couple took the job permanently.

Mrs. Garcia was to pack her personal belongings and return to Antonito the next day on 478's coach with Father O'Flanigan and Mr. Yang. The Father had told her parents, who would be expecting her.

She wondered, of course, about Eli. She had a special feeling for this man who would care so much about her. She learned he was the prime suspect in Leo's death, and of course, later heard he'd been arrested and was in jail in Conejos.

She worried for poor Willie Estrada, who'd been so scared he'd run away again. She wasn't that surprised. Willie couldn't stand the pressure, and there was little else for him to do, or so he probably thought, and she understood that. She'd been around Willie too much not to.

Her family, who'd recently moved to Conejos, took her in, and she, in turn, took in laundry to help them with the added expense of her being back home. Her work life didn't get much more comfortable, but her bruises healed. It would take more time for her mental scars to mend, but for the most part, they eventually would. Some of the neighbors gave her what she called 'the look' for what they believed was her complicity in the affair for what it was. But they'd learned of her mistreatment since her marriage had begun and they more or less forgave her.

She paid attention to the news of Eli's arrest. She learned that he'd threatened to kill Leo in front of at least three different people, all reliable and with no ax to grind. Arriana knew that two of them, Sam Gonzales and Jose Villela, were Eli's best buddies. *With them as friends*, thought Arri, *he sure didn't need any enemies.*

Could she have misunderstood a certain gentleness she'd thought she felt in Eli or was he just like the rest? Or at least her understanding of the rest?

Arriana did not try to visit Eli in jail but sent and received some messages through Father O'Flanigan. Eli replied through the priest, saying he hoped she was well and was sorry for how he'd helped unravel her life, but his intentions had been honorable, at least. She told Father O'Flanigan only to tell Eli she thought of him and was sorry he faced what he did.

31

MAKING SENSE OF IT

Southern Colorado and northern New Mexico were a part of Spain beginning in the 1500s then a part of Mexico when that country declared its independence from Spain in 1821. Many of the early settlers were of Spanish origin. Many came from the Bosque region of Spain; thus, sheepherding was something they traditionally knew, and it became an integral part of their way of life. More so than cattle raising though both were important.

Spain and then Mexico made many land grants to their influential citizens to settle the land, bring civilization to it. For example, in 1832, Manuel Martinez of Abiquiu, New Mexico, was given 500,000 acres between Chama and Antonito and to the south in what was known as the Tierra Amarilla land grant.

The United States and Mexico went to war in 1846. The US prevailed, and a peace treaty, the Treaty of Guadalupe Hidalgo, was signed in 1848 when the war ended. Part of that treaty required the US to recognize the ownership of land under grants in which the owner had complied with all its conditions. Mr. Martinez had done so. So private ownership of the property along the Denver & Rio Grande Western was in place in 1927, substantially the portion of the route west of Cumbres Pass over to Chama.

Also in the Treaty of Guadalupe Hidalgo was an original provision that the US pay Mexico $15 million for what would later become the states of California, Arizona, New Mexico, and portions of southern Colorado. The latter included the San Luis Valley and the towns already in existence, like Conejos.

Colorado and New Mexico initially became territories of the United States. Later they became states. Colorado became the 38th state of the union in 1876, New Mexico, the 47th state but not until 1912. The citizens of both states embraced their new country with great patriotism!

In 1898, the United States went to war with Spain over Cuba. It was the first major overseas military adventure for the young US. Colonel Teddy Roosevelt wanted the best men for his Rough Riders, those who would fight in Cuba. He believed that men of Colorado, New Mexico, and Texas, who knew how to ride, shoot, and fight as well as anyone, were perhaps the best suited.

Therefore, the Southwest provided many of the soldiers who gained fame in Cuba, winning against the Spanish as Teddy's men stormed up San Juan Hill, the final battle. Great pride developed in Colorado and New Mexico and other regions of the Southwest over this achievement. The Rough Riders were welcomed home, heroes!

World War I came along, and soldiers from the

Southwest performed admirably. Denver & Rio Grande Western foreman, Leo Garcia of Sublette, was one of those decorated. Patriotism was rampant in 1927. July 4th celebrations were a significant event in every small and large town. Politicians made speeches. Fireworks exploded, and cannons boomed that had been used in those wars and returned to some of those towns to adorn the town square. Artillerymen who knew how to use them, who'd fired them in combat, discharged blanks on patriotic holidays. It was an honor to be a member of the 'big gun' team.

In Antonito, Colorado, an artillery piece from the war with Spain adorned the square. Private Thomas Ganaan, a Rough Rider veteran, was the main artillery-man who operated it. His assistant gunner was Corporal Joseph Vigil, like Leo, a veteran of World War I. The Antonito cannon, when shot, could be heard throughout the lower half of the San Luis Valley, and the citizens were proud of its thunderous boom.

After his sentencing, Eli Martinez thought many times about the last look he'd have of his beloved San Luis Valley. Mr. Ferguson, who'd been the first and to date the only person hung out there six miles west of Antonito, had had such a view, and Eli hoped that the accused man had thought it a fitting place to die if there was one.

Thus Eli had one request in court on October 7th when sentenced. "Let me die on my locomotive, in the manner of Mr. Ferguson. If you're going to take my life, hang me at Ferguson's Trestle. I've worked hard to make the San Luis Valley a better place. My family name has been an honorable one. Please grant me this one last wish."

The judge considered it. An unusual request, but

Colorado was still what many in the eastern United States thought of like the Wild West. Why not? Eli's family was a good one. This crazy situation was the only blemish. Eliseo Martinez had been a positive part of the Denver & Rio Grande Western, which had brought success and prosperity to the area. He was a highly trained engineer. His favorite locomotive was the K-36 type, the 480 series, and surely one would be available in the Antonito yards.

The judge had his bailiff inquire. Yes, the '87 would be there, and the railroad agreed to reserve it.

"Okay, Mr. Martinez. We can allow that. A week from today, on October 14th, your sentence will be carried out at Ferguson's Trestle. You will hang from the # 487, one of the K-36 locomotives. May God have mercy on your soul."

The sentencing day was a hard one for the southern part of the San Luis Valley, in reality, for all of Colorado up to Denver and at least the northern part of New Mexico. Both the murderer and victim were outstanding in their way.

Eli was a star engineer. He had many relatives who lived nearby. His life had been exemplary to this point. As a young boy, growing up in Conejos, Colorado, he'd attended Our Lady of Guadalupe church, the oldest in the state. Father Terrence O'Flanigan thought the world of Eli or certainly had until now.

Eli had served as an altar boy while attending the church. He knew the difference between right and wrong. Eliseo knew what a murderer faced in the afterlife if God had not been sincerely asked for forgiveness. He was a responsible person and would never disrespect his family name.

He had always been an achiever in all ways. He'd been engaged to Maria Lopez, though he'd given that up, for the greater good, he thought, certainly for her greater good. And her life was working out well, and Eli knew she was happy.

He loved Arri and wanted to protect her. He knew that loving a married woman was wrong in itself, but he also knew that Leo Garcia was wrong to treat her in the cruel way he did. Where was justice? Where was the balance? It was all mind-boggling. And he knew he was innocent, or so he believed. Even now, he sometimes was confused. Could he have let his anger overcome his good judgment? Could he have temporarily gone insane? He thought he knew the answers to those questions but sometimes was uncertain when he dwelled on them.

Eliseo Martinez wasn't a war hero like Leo Garcia; he'd just been a year or so too young when the World War I draft occurred, or he'd have been chosen to go also. Now Eli regretted not having lied about his age and served. He would have done his best, though he, like so many others, may not have come home. Better that, however, than being hanged to death in front of so many people you knew and loved. It was so disgraceful, and not like him. But he supposed he would have done anything to protect Arriana; maybe he was guilty and didn't know it.

And then there was Leo Garcia. Leo was a valuable worker for the Denver & Rio Grande Western, which meant so much to the San Luis Valley. He was a war hero, although Leo had known some things he never admitted to others about the circumstances of his survival the day that Alvin York went crazy, as he'd seen it, and killed all those German boys. And of course about how he'd lived through all the days that led up to that one. A lot of his fellow soldiers had died and helped Leo live as their dead bodies were used for cover to stop enemy bullets. But a man had to be smart in battle, right? If you just walked out there, you were going to die.

Leo had been confident there were his equals on the enemy side, Germans who'd survived through horrible days when their friends had not. Leo had thought about all that while he lived.

He'd been a good foreman for the railroad, a man who helped keep the train running through weather rain or shine. He'd been tough; you had to be to do his job. He'd provided for Arriana, who had few options. The Public didn't know the extent of his mistreatment of her. There had been rumors, but many of the men who heard those stories had a dark record of their own regarding such treatment of women.

Leo's wife had not had to be a RW, a railroad woman; not a laundress who worked hard hours every day to have something to eat. She had a warm place to live, food to eat, a nice-enough house. That was more than many possessed, and it was Leo whose work skills and effort had provided those things.

Leo was a star in his way, as was Eli Martinez. People were perplexed. What had pushed Eli off the deep end? They understood love but couldn't understand how this thing had gone so wrong.

Many went to Our Lady of Guadalupe church – lit candles – prayed – talked to Father O'Flanigan about all of it. The only thing Father could tell them was that sometimes stars in the universe, even though God-created, sometimes collided with disastrous results.

One of those collisions seemed to be at hand.

32

MODEL T RIDER

For anything as serious as a hanging, Sheriff Lee liked to plan for whatever might happen. No appeal was filed for Eli, but Colorado Governor Donald Harris still had the right to issue a last-minute reprieve based on any late information that came to his attention.

How could they be prepared for that in the unlikely event it might happen, since the execution was to take place out on Ferguson's Trestle, nearly six miles from Antonito? The nearest telephone box, which also still had a telegraph key in it, was a mile farther west. The sheriff discussed it with railroad officials in Antonito. Notification, if it happened, would come by telegraph. And the depot could also immediately reach the telephone handset, which was in the old telegraph booth.

Sheriff Lee had two deputies who were telegraph operators. It was useful to have them trained. If they were in the railroad station or elsewhere a telegraph key was clicking, they could listen for themselves what was being said instead of depending on the operator to tell them. The railroad could be a little tricky with guarding their information, and the practice had proven beneficial.

Sheriff Lee decided to post one of them, William Smith, at the telephone box that one mile west of Ferguson's Trestle. Smitty's telegraph skills shouldn't be needed, but you never knew. Smitty was being sent there to signal a halt to the hanging if the word was received to do so. The indication would be three rifle shots. It was a short distance over which to hear. The deputy was to wait a minute then fire another three shots. When the sound of those gunshots reached the trestle, they'd answer with three shots from the locomotive so Smitty would know they'd gotten the message. Understanding the three answering shots, he'd then pick up the telephone handset and advise the railroad: Execution stopped.

No one could ever be sure the telephone wire might not be down due to high winds or other adverse weather or other failures. So Sheriff Lee's back-up plan involved the artillery piece in the Antonito town square. The two regular artillerymen would be stationed there as they were on official holidays when they fired the cannon. Sure, it was six miles out to the hanging site, but the sound of the big gun could easily reach that distance up the canyon towards Lava Tank. To make sure, he had the men test-fire the cannon with Smitty out at the trestle. No problem, easily heard, reported the deputy.

If a message were received either at the Antonito railroad station or the Sheriff's Office, halting or delaying the hanging, a fast car would deliver it to the town square. The Conejos Sheriff's office had two Model T's, one to be placed at each location. Practice of the procedure took place. It was a three-minute drive from each site to the square where the big gun was. Sheriff Lee told no one, but he planned to delay the hanging at least five minutes past 6 am, the time set by the judge, to cover the bases. He would set his pocket watch five minutes slow.

Eliseo Martinez was a local boy who had always been a good man, a reputable man, and incidentally had many relatives and friends who would vote in November. Sheriff Lee hoped it would still be for him.

The sheriff didn't like this whole deal and didn't want it to get fouled up in any way beyond the normal crazy thing it already was.

If the execution were to be halted, the artillerymen were to fire three rounds when they received a message to that regard. Otherwise, they were to keep the gun silent. Sheriff Lee had been around long enough to know that nothing in life could guarantee that old Mr. Murphy wouldn't intervene, but this ought to do it. Down not too deep, he hoped he'd hear three rifle shots or three booms of the cannon, though he didn't see it happening that close to the deadline.

Wait there by the Pearly Gate, Eli, he mused, *we'll all get there soon enough, you'll just be a little earlier than the rest of us.* The sheriff figured Eli was having Pearly Gate thoughts of his own about now.

Sheriff Lee had been thinking of all this at his office when Smitty walked by. "It's a strange world we live in," said the sheriff to Smitty, who didn't know precisely what strange thing his boss was talking about, but having been a deputy for 23 years, heartily agreed.

"You are correct about that, Sheriff," replied Smitty,

who at that moment was thinking about his upcoming seven-mile horseback ride out to the telephone box.

Smitty wasn't lazy but was starting to like riding around in the Model T's, compared to bouncing around on his horse.

He wasn't on the horse yet and drove one of the T's over to the little stone Antonito depot to see when the last freight was scheduled to pass by the telephone box. Maybe he could put himself and the horse on the train and get off there.

Smitty hadn't lasted those 23 years in this job without doing some thinking.

33

A MAN OF HONOR

A hanging wouldn't usually draw national attention but the hanging of a railroad engineer from his locomotive, at his request? Well, that was different, and the prominent newspapers and magazines ate it up. A picture of Eliseo Martinez, along with a photo of engine # 487 from which he'd be hung, had circulated the country.

Stories got around fast in 1927, although it wasn't immediate, of course.

John Sampson, Willie's new boss, was proud that he could read. And he knew that train passengers passing through San Diego often discarded papers at the depot. After a long day, Sampson would walk the short two blocks to the station and collect one, bring it home, and see what the news was. Thus Willie Estrada, who stayed in a small room at the back of the stable, happened to walk by Mr. Sampson's office on October 15th when he saw a picture in a newspaper of a locomotive with a man standing in front of it.

Willie couldn't read, but he sure could recognize

things and people in a picture. *Oh, my goodness! It was engineer Eli Martinez in front of the '87! What did the writing part say?*

Willie asked Mr. Sampson what the newspaper said about the man. Willie didn't admit to recognizing the person or knowing anything about the engine but said he'd been around trains and was curious.

Sampson told Willie that the man in the photograph was a Colorado train engineer and was to be hung off the smokestack of his locomotive, that # 487. It was to happen at his asking. He'd killed a railroad man named Leo Garcia over a love affair with Garcia's wife, and the day-old paper reported the hanging would take place on October 14th.

Suddenly Willie had trouble breathing. "What day is it?" asked a shocked Willie. They would hang Eli for killing Leo Garcia, that wasn't right! Willie knew that Eli had not killed Mr. Garcia; he was there when it all happened. If anybody had killed Mr. Garcia, it had been me, thought Willie Estrada, and no one else. As far as he could reason out, Willie believed that Leo Garcia had pretty much killed himself.

"What day is it, Mr. Sampson?" begged Willie again, beside himself.

"If you're worried about that engineer, Willie, forget it. Today is October 15th. He went over the river yesterday morning. May God have mercy on his soul," replied John Sampson.

Willie was devastated. He left the stable, walked around. What could be done? Could he live with this? If Willie couldn't save Eli's life, he could at least tell the world that Mr. Martinez had been an innocent man. By running away, Willie Estrada had gotten the engineer killed. He should have stayed. Guilt ate away at him and quickly.

He knew that a San Diego city policeman was posted at the train station, two blocks away. He ran over there, taking the newspaper with him.

Willie found the officer, showed him the picture. Willie was frantic and seemed genuinely remorseful though his ladder seemed to be leaning slightly against the wrong wall.

"I knew this engineer. I worked on this train. I know this locomotive. This man, Eliseo Martinez, didn't kill Leo Garcia. I did! I need to turn myself in, so the people back in Colorado know he was innocent," cried Willie, literally sobbing, near hysterical.

Officer Danny Lewis had seen some strange things in his time but thought, well, I may have a loony on my hands, but he seems to know about the man and the train, so I'd better take him down to the station. At the San Diego Police Department, Detective Billy Hook had night duty.

Detective Hook listened to Estrada's account, sensed there was something to it. But there was no great hurry since the execution of engineer Martinez happened yesterday. He would take down all the information, make out a report, and give it to his boss, who could authorize Hook to send it to Colorado if it seemed genuine. They could hold Estrada on suspicion, and await word from Colorado.

"Tell me what happened, Estrada, all of it," said Hook. Willie opened up with what sounded like a believable story. Why would a man who couldn't read confess to a murder that happened way across the country? Made no sense to lie about it.

Willie got to the part where he'd been standing over the gorge with Leo Garcia, Mr. Garcia balancing precariously on the rail over the drop-off. There were other men there, Willie explained, who must have seen it too. Mr. Garcia had cursed Eli Martinez, called him a bastard to his face, and Mr. Martinez had turned to step away from Garcia. Willie was close enough to touch them both. He told the detective this was what had happened:

"When Mr. Martinez turned and started to walk away, Leo Garcia reached into his right back pocket where he always carried a ball-peen hammer. He pulled the hammer out and yelled: You bastard! Mr. Garcia raised his right arm to hit Mr. Martinez in the head with it. I couldn't let that happen and reached out with my left arm to stop him, and he hit my arm here with his arm – he showed Detective Hook his left forearm – and that threw him off-balance, and he went over backward in the gorge. I saw the bottom of his shoes flip up. He made a horrible scream going down. He had been good to me in his way, and his wife Arriana had been very good to me, and there was no way I could have killed him on purpose, but I couldn't let him kill Mr. Martinez. I ran away because I was scared of being asked about all of it. Now Mr. Martinez is dead, killed for something he did not do. Please let the people in Colorado know that Mr. Martinez was not a bad man!"

Hmmmmm, thought Detective Hook, this sounds legit, could be something to it. This man knows too much.

At the heart of things, being an experienced officer, Detective Hook was a cynic like nearly all policemen. He knew he heard only Estrada's part of a story. In spite of his cynicism, though, Hook thought that if this story was the truth – and he was inclined to believe it – the train engineer in Colorado had caught a horrible break. But the fact was he was powerless to stop what had already happened. At the least, however, maybe Martinez's name could be cleared. Only fair.

He wrote up a statement and had Willie sign it, well, affix his mark to it witnessed by himself and Officer Lewis. Hook wouldn't see the Chief of Detectives until the next night, and the man in Colorado was already dead, so no hurry in getting the message off. The following evening, Detective Hook's boss reviewed and signed it, then Billy walked it up to the police dispatcher's office to the telegraph key operator. It was nearly 4 am, almost 5 am in Colorado, October 16th.

"What's the priority, Billy?" asked the telegrapher, Miss Debbie Zinsmeister. "Well, damn shame, Deb, but just make it Routine, too bad, but it's a case of too little, too late," replied the detective. "I know your office is under the gun like ours to save a nickel when we can." Billy knew that an Urgent message was 50 cents more. The telegrapher said it had been a long night, and she was going across the street to a little café for coffee and a donut. Miss Zinsmeister would get the wire on the way before leaving work at 7 am. She didn't like to leave unfinished paperwork for the person who relieved her.

Willie Estrada was placed in a jail cell in San Diego, awaiting word from Colorado as to what to do with him.

Willie may have been a simple man, but he was a man of honor. Every day since his 22nd birthday, he'd kept his pants up with a leather belt that was engraved – 'From Arriana with love.'

The belt had been given to Leo Garcia on their wedding day by his new wife in hopes of a happy marriage. Later, when Leo outgrew it, at a time when little waste of valuable things took place, Arriana Garcia had given it to Willie for being so willing to help her after he'd already done a hard day's work.

Ordinarily, such a belt would have been removed from a prisoner, but the San Diego police jailer had made an exception in Willie Estrada's case since he seemed to be such a nice person, a bit simple-minded perhaps, but someone you couldn't help but like. He was being held 'just in case,' and if he was a murderer, he had owned up to it, and would probably get away with it anyway due to his mental state. The police had contacted a shocked John Sampson and assured him they would treat Willie well, and in fact, he could help as a trustee outside the cell until the matter was cleared up.

That night, a little before dawn, a distraught Willie Estrada, who couldn't live with himself knowing that Eli Martinez had died for something he did not do, hung himself in his jail cell, using the leather belt he cherished.

San Diego Police immediately sent the Conejos County, Colorado, Sheriff's Office another telegram telling them of the suicide.

From Arriana with love, indeed.

34

JUST LIKE CHOPPING WOOD

Thursday, October 13th. The day before Eli Martinez's date with the hangman, he'd waited anxiously in his cell. Father O'Flanigan visited. Eli's family waited and prayed and lit candles in Our Lady of Guadalupe Church. The priest already had a grave dug for Eli. Both the sheriff and Smitty dropped by the jail and said: "Sorry this is happening, Eli, you're a good man."

On the night before Eliseo Martinez's hanging, Arriana Garcia suddenly felt compelled to try to stop it or delay it, who knew what the result might be?

She limped down the one-mile stretch of road to the Antonito yards, where she knew # 487, scheduled for use in Eli's execution, stood fired up in the engine shops. She crawled under a fence away from where the night watchman, old man Rathbone, spent most of his time. She found the '87 steaming, located a sledgehammer nearby, and climbed the ladder into the cab.

She found herself spitting out "Leo!" as she swung the eight-pound hammer at controls and instruments she understood to be essential to the locomotive's operation. She knew the sight-glasses and gauges were all needed, and she singled them out. It's your fault this happened, Leo Garcia, she thought, take that!

She also knew that Mr. Rathbone would hear the noise and come running, as running as a 75-year-old man could. But she easily outdistanced and evaded him while running back to her parents' house. Arriana cried all night. For the moment, there was nothing more she could do.

About 10 pm on October 13ᵗʰ, the Denver & Rio Grande Western Antonito yard contacted the sheriff's office. "We got a problem," they told Sheriff Lee, who was close at hand.

"Just after dark, the night watchman was up by the depot and heard some hammering back in the shop where # 487, steamed and ready for tomorrow, was stored. He didn't think anybody was back there working but went over to check. He saw a small person running away from the '87, and he chased the person, but Rathbone is an older man and lost whoever it was in the dark. All he can tell us is that it looked like the person had hurt themselves somehow, seemed to have a limp."

"Whoever it was got in the '87's cab and worked over the controls with a sledgehammer, busted out all the gauges. The engine won't be moving; we'll have to let her steam down. But there's no other 480 series available between here and Chama on the west side and Colorado Springs over here east. We need a delay if we're to obey the judge's order to hang Eli Martinez from a K-36."

Well, hell's bells, thought Sheriff Lee, *how much agony can one man take*, with Eli Martinez in mind. But the railroad was right; the sheriff now had to notify the judge of the situation. There had been all this national publicity.

The judge had a one-word comment. "Damn!"

He thought about it quickly and made up his mind. He ordered a two-day delay; the hanging would not take place until 48 hours later, at 6 am on October 16th. The Public had to be satisfied.

Locally, the word spread quickly that Eli's hanging was delayed two days since the planned locomotive had been damaged, and another one wasn't immediately available. Arriana wasn't surprised and thought, *Oh, darn. That was so easy I might do it again. Good thing that Leo always had me chopping wood with that heavy ax.*

It would be hard to say that Eli Martinez was happy with the delay, but when life is precious, at its end time, who wouldn't choose to have another 48 hours? Sometimes there is no choice in a matter, and Eli had none.

At daybreak, October 16, 1927, all was in readiness at Ferguson's Trestle. Eli Martinez had a final moment with Father O'Flanigan. Eli didn't feel he had a lot of sins to confess, but he took advantage of the opportunity to get Angel and Gloria off his conscience. *Eli, you surprise me,* reflected Father O'Flanigan, *but you're just human, after all.*

Eli refused a hood. He'd have his last moment on earth looking at his beloved San Luis Hills in the near distance, the Sangre de Cristo way out to the east. Mount Blanca, over 14,000 feet tall, one of 53 peaks in Colorado called Fourteeners, was to his left, clearly visible. He could even make out those high sand dunes at its base.

The '88 had come in from Chama. It was the engine Eli had driven to Rock Tunnel that fateful day.

Might as well see this all the way through, it might have been thinking. The railroad, ever open to profit no matter the situation, and believing 'Why Not?' since the hanging would happen regardless, had sold more than 300 tickets to people who'd ridden coaches, even flatcars, to a once in a lifetime event. People wanted those front row seats. About a fourth of the riders were reporters.

Smitty had watched the train roll by his position a mile west, with the curious aboard. "Damn them," he muttered out loud, to no one in particular.

Eli and the sheriff and others, including Father O'Flanigan, had been brought out in the early-morning darkness in a coach, a K-27 pulling it. A covered pine box was in the back of the coach. The artillerymen were in place in the Antonito town square, just in case.

Eli stood perched on the ties of Ferguson's Trestle, a hangman's noose around his neck, the top fastened over the smokestack of the '88, those in attendance wondering whether the rope would catch on fire. Somehow it didn't though it was smoking and wouldn't last too long. The thoroughly-prepared Sheriff Lee had another noose in the coach, just in case.

The sheriff cocked his ears, straining to hear over the noise of the locomotive. He'd forgotten just how loud even a stationary K-36 was sitting idle. *Uh oh, detail missed.*

Eli thought about family, the good life he'd had, the good times. Too bad those things were coming to an end so soon. He asked God once more for forgiveness for any sins not previously confessed, though he did not ask for forgiveness for killing Leo Garcia since he had not, so far as Eliseo knew.

And yes, Eli thought about Arriana. He could have loved her for a lifetime.

But mostly, he considered Ferguson, on whose trestle he stood. Had a mistake been made, could Ferguson have been an innocent too? He hoped that Ferguson had loved and appreciated the San Luis Valley as he had. Many people say: I know how you feel when they don't. But Eli felt the same emotional pain he believed Ferguson must have experienced.

The sheriff had been right. *Meet me at the gate, Ferguson*, Eli thought. *We'll have something to discuss, for sure. Guess I'll see you in a couple of minutes*, he reckoned. His fatalistic thoughts were suddenly interrupted.

KABOOM! KABOOM! KABOOM!

From the direction of Antonito...

Sheriff Lee and everyone else, including Arriana, who was in Conejos just a mile away, heard the big gun.

All of them knew by now of the not-so-secret plan to have the cannon fire if the sheriff received a last-minute reprieve, though no one expected to hear it.

God must have had a hand in this, Arri thought, as she limped and ran the mile to the Antonito station. There, she'd heard the news, which didn't take long to spread in a small town.

The Conejos County Sheriff's Office had just received two back to back telegrams from the San Diego, California, Police Department.

In the first, at 5:50 am Colorado time, a statement from a Willie Estrada, age 22, who claimed to have witnessed the death of one Leo Garcia on August 20, 1927, near Osier, Colorado, contained information clearing Eli Martinez of the murder of Garcia. Newspapers reported Martinez's upcoming execution by hanging set for October 14, 1927, for complicity in Garcia's death. "Estrada's information appears to be credible. Estrada being held in custody pending your advice soonest, his full signed/witnessed statement attached." Signed, Wally Anderson, Chief of Detectives at the San Diego Police Department, San Diego, California, dated October 16, 1927.

The second received just minutes later informed that before the morning headcount this date, a jailer had found Willie Estrada dead in his cell, having hanged himself. The same official signed it.

Poor Willie was somehow the key person involved

in Leo's death, and he'd taken his life way out in California because of it, Arriana thought. She wouldn't get details for a while. But she also heard that Willie's confession had cleared Eli. Eli was innocent!

She was very sad to learn about Willie but would have more details of his death soon. Right now, she wondered about Eli.

Did he still want her? This much she knew for sure. She'd be right there in Antonito when he returned to find out!

At the trestle, a few seconds after the cannon fired, three distinctive cracks of a Winchester '94 rifle sounded from another direction.

The sheriff fired his .30-.30 three times in reply, then heard another three rounds.

"Stop this mess!" he shouted to all.

Sheriff Lee unshackled Eli. The sheriff figured Smitty had gotten a telephone or telegraph message back at the booth a mile away.

A speeder was at the back of # 488's consist and raced to find Smitty, who was already galloping their direction, wishing he had the Model T.

"Eli's been cleared, Sheriff! Willie Estrada was found in California and confessed he did it. Willie killed himself, Eli is a free man!"

"Damn, son," said Sheriff Lee, smiling and calmly turning to Eli, lifting the noose from around his neck, untying his hands. "You sure like to cut 'em close. What say you get behind the wheel of the '88 here and take us back to town? I'm buying."

The sheriff immediately felt better about his reelection chances.

One mile out, at the Antonito yard limit sign, Eli

sounded his signature whistle. The first note said: AaaaaaaaaaahRiiiiiiiiiiiiiiiiiiiiiiI!

At the stone depot, it seemed half the town was waiting. But Eli Martinez saw only one face, front and center.

It was Arriana's.

EPILOGUE

When the search team fired the three-shot salute to war hero Leo Garcia in Toltec Gorge on August 21, 1927, the sound echoed off the walls of the universe. In the land beyond the stars, a ghostly company of WWI doughboys finally relaxed, knowing that God's perfect plan of justice had worked again, though Sgt Garcia could have modified the plan by asking forgiveness. He had not.

Garcia had caused his own death while trying to kill another, a reversal of the role that had spared his life during the Great War when he'd hastened the demise of so many of his comrades.

Willie Estrada's body was returned from California and buried in the grave prepared for Eliseo Martinez. The belt was in Willie's coffin. The crowd was huge.

A cedar tombstone, carved by Adrian Macheco, was placed on the gravesite. It said: Guillermo 'Willie" Estrada 1905 – 1927 Man of Honor

In November, voters reelected Sheriff Juan Lee in a landslide.

Eli and Arriana were married a year after Leo Garcia's death.

Division 4 superintendent Mr. Hawkins gave them a sledgehammer for a wedding present, saying they should use it together when they had problems to work out.

They bought the little Chama house and became regular members of St. Michael's Catholic Church.

They had a boy named Willie, no surprise. He was called Junior. Later, their little girl was christened Cynthia Louise, the first names of their mothers, but was known to all as Cindy Lou.

Eli worked for the Denver & Rio Grande Western for 30 more years, driving the last westbound passenger train, the San Juan Express, on January 31, 1951. His final trip as an engineer was that same route on a freight, February 19, 1957, in locomotive # 489.

He always maintained his signature whistle. Some say the sound of it still bounces off canyon walls in the San Juan Mountains. AaaaaaaaaaahRiiiiiiiiiiiiiiiiiiiii!

Eli said a prayer for the soul of Willie Estrada each time he drove by Toltec Gorge, and yes, for Leo Garcia's soul too.

Arri and Eli listened to the music of the trains for the rest of their lives.

Arriana preceded Eli in death by six weeks. When she passed away, Eli lost his will to live. "I just want to be with Arri," he told a friend.

He is. And their earthly remains are together in Our Lady of Guadalupe Cemetery in Conejos, Colorado.

Next to Willie Estrada, their friend.

THANKS FOR READING!

The Denver & Rio Grande ran both passenger and freight trains from 1881 through 1951. The Colorado Express (eastbound) and New Mexico Express (westbound) passenger trains were renamed the San Juan Express in 1937. Freight service only continued until 1967, with the line abandoned in 1968.

At various times throughout its history, it had these mottos: Through the Rockies, Not Around Them; Main Line through the Rockies; The Action Railroad; and Scenic Line of the World.

All were appropriate!

In 1970, the states of Colorado and New Mexico purchased the remaining 64 miles of track between Antonito, Colorado, and Chama, New Mexico. The line, now called the Cumbres & Toltec Scenic Railroad, has operated as a tourist train since.

The C&TSRR, designated a National Historic Landmark in 2012, continues to carry on with a dedicated staff, some in their fifth generation of service. Volunteers who love both history and trains work during the summers to restore equipment and interpret the railroad's history to visitors. It is my honor to serve as a docent.

Help is always needed. You can be a part of keeping our railroad in business by volunteering. No matter your skillset, you will be valuable in preserving this living, working museum for others! Visit our Friends website at www.cumbrestoltec.org or write Friends of the Cumbres & Toltec Scenic Railroad, Inc., 4421 McLeod Rd NE Suite F, Albuquerque, New Mexico 87109 to learn more.

Ticket and schedule information and additional facts about the train may be found at www.cumbrestoltec. com or by calling 1-888-286-2737.

Of 20 scenic train rides in North America, voters in national surveys consistently place the C&TSRR in the top tier. It is among the leading tourist attractions in both Colorado and New Mexico. Riding behind our Baldwin steam engines is a "bucket list" experience. The fall aspen color season is a special thing to behold. Treat yourself and share it with us!

My sincere thanks to Cynthia, my wife, for her support. Also, to these special people who helped with editing and suggestions: Adriana R. Ortiz, Debbie Butler, Joy Owen, Roberta Martinez, and Suzie Martin. My appreciation to the Osterwald family who publishes "Ticket to Toltec" for information gained from Bible-like study of their excellent book in connection with my docent duties!

Your comments are welcome, and you may contact me at www.billyandersauthor.com. To God be the glory, great things He has done.

Billy Anders

DEDICATION

This book is dedicated to the memory of a brave 10-year-old boy, still remembered after many years.

On April 22, 1976, I was working as a police helicopter pilot in San Antonio, Texas. My flying partner was Detective Bob Garnett. We were dispatched to a rural area of the city to search for a missing Hispanic youngster.

An intruder had murdered the boy's grandparents and sister during a home-invasion type burglary. Homicide officers found three victims inside the house, but the 10-year-old was missing. The property consisted of several acres, much of it brushy.

During a systematic aerial search, we located his body about 300 yards northeast of the home. It was evident that he'd been running for his life. He lay facedown, shot in the back of the head. He faced in the direction of the freedom he'd so desperately hoped to find. It was in the top three of the saddest things I saw during 31 years in law enforcement.

The investigation pointed to a responsible person. He was a Mexican national, illegally in our country. He fled to Los Angeles, California, where he was arrested and incarcerated, awaiting extradition.

Fiction is fiction, but of course, real-life experiences are called on to write fictional stories. While imprisoned, the murderer hung himself in his California jail cell. Did he finally accept responsibility? Did he have a bit of honor, after all? One can only hope. Any comparison of his character to this story's Willie Estrada, a man of real honor, is not intended.

What I have always remembered is the incredible courage displayed by the small boy, who did all he could to live against impossible odds. This event occurred in just the second year of my career. He inspired me always to do my best to keep my law enforcement oath to protect life and property.

Not many people know of that little guy's bravery. Now you do. Live some for him, won't you?

Rest in peace, Jovincito Valiente. You are not forgotten.

CPSIA information can be obtained
at www.ICGtesting.com
Printed in the USA
BVHW090348111121
621204BV00009B/628